BY KATHLEEN KARR

MAN OF THE FAMILY

KATHLEEN KARR

Man of the Family

Family

Farrar, Straus and Giroux

NEW YORK

The translation of Sándor Petöfi's "National Song,"
which appears on pages 76–77, is adapted from translations
of the poem by Edwin Morgan in Rebel or Revolutionary?:
Sándor Petöfi, As Revealed by His Diary, Letters, Notes,
Pamphlets and Poems (Budapest: Corvina Press, 1974) and by Anton
N. Nyerges in Petöfi, edited by Joseph M. Értavy-Baráth (Buffalo:
Hungarian Cultural Foundation, 1974). Grateful acknowledgment
to Corvina Press and A. Endre Nyerges for permission.

Distributed in Canada by Douglas & McIntyre Ltd.
Printed in the United States of America
Designed by Judy Lanfredi
First edition, 1999
3 5 7 9 11 10 8 6 4 2

Library of Congress Cataloging-in-Publication Data
Karr, Kathleen.
    Man of the family / Kathleen Karr. — 1st ed.
    p.   cm.
    Summary: During the 1920s, life for Istvan, the eldest child of a
Hungarian-American family, holds both joy and sadness.
    ISBN 0-374-34764-6
    1. Hungarian Americans—Juvenile fiction.   [1. Hungarian
Americans—Fiction.   2. Fathers and sons—Fiction.   3. Family
life—New Jersey—Fiction.   4. New Jersey—Fiction.]   I. Title.
PZ7.K149Man   1999
[Fic]—dc21   99-26051

In memory of my father
Stephen Csere
(1914–1996)

and my grandfather
Michael Csere
(1881–1924)

GLOSSARY

Here's a guide to the Hungarian names and words used in this book.

ANYA (*On-ya*): mother

APA (*Ah-pa*): father

BÉLA (*BAY-la*)

CSÁNGO (*CHANG-o*): a person coming from a certain region of the Carpathian mountains

CSERE (*char-a*)

CZARDAS (*cha-dash*): a joyous Hungarian dance that starts slowly, then builds to rapid whirls

EGÉSZSÉGÉRE (*egg-ee-chay-ger-a*): a toast: "To your health!"

GULYÁS (*goo-losh*): a thick soup with stew meat and lots of paprika, Hungarian red pepper

ISTENEM (*EESH-ten-em*): God

ISTVÁN (*EESHT-von*)

KALÁCS (*cull-ach*): a cake whose dough is first rolled out flat and covered with jam, then rolled back up again and baked

KIFLI (*kiff-lee*): a cookie pastry shaped like the crescent moon, with very light, flaky dough, and a filling of jam or nuts and raisins

LEKVÁR (*lek-var*): prune jam

MAGYAR (*Mudge-are*): Hungarian

MIHÁLY (*Mee-high*)

NAGYON FINOM (*nudge-un FEE-nom*): delicious, very fine

PALACSINTA (*pal-a-chin-ta*): Hungarian pancakes, which are thin and closer to French crêpes than American pancakes

PISTA (*PEESH-ta*)

SÁNDOR (*Shon-dore*)

SZERVUSZ (*serve-oos*): a greeting: "Hi!"

MAN OF THE FAMILY

ONE

Mom wasn't beautiful, but Pop thought she was.

Those were the names I called my parents later, after I learned proper English in school. But when I was a small boy they were *Anya* and *Apa*.

Anya *was* pretty, though I didn't realize it then. She wore her long pale hair differently from other ladies'. It was pulled away from her heart-shaped face and piled up in the back, kind of fancy. That was just the way it looked in her wedding picture that sat on the mantel in the parlor. The style was old-fashioned for 1924, but Apa liked it that way.

Apa didn't have much hair at all, just a little dark

fuzz on top, much thicker on the sides. But he had a glorious mustache that made up for this lack. It was black and thick and luxurious, and curled down at the ends toward his strong square jaw. He had more hair in the wedding picture. That was taken eleven long years back, though, and on the other side of the ocean, in Hungary.

"Sea voyages, István," Apa often said to me, "can be difficult."

To me those words meant that something in the ocean water, or maybe the trade winds, had snatched his hair during that long-ago crossing. When he said this, I always felt for my own pale thatch with worry. If Apa could lose his hair so easily, maybe I could, too. It didn't make me anxious to take to the sea.

But there was not much fear of that. We lived inland, on the flat plains of South Jersey. The ocean was an impossible twenty miles away. Impossible, because we didn't have the fares for a train excursion. We owned no vehicle, either. Not a sturdy Model T Ford, as some of the neighbors had acquired. Not a horse and wagon. Not even a bicycle. We owned only our legs. In short, we were poor.

I was thinking about these things one day while I was tending our farm. It was spring, and the vegetable garden had just been planted between the back of the house and the chicken coop. It was my job to keep the chickens out of it until a fence could be built. This was a reasonable job for a boy. Unfortunately, since I was ten and the oldest, it was also my job to keep my brothers and sister in line. That meant not only out of the garden but also as far as possible from the scrabbling hens, who'd as soon peck at baby Béla as at the nearest bug.

Sándor, two years younger than me, was hardly ever a problem. He was always across the dirt road poking into the old car our equally impoverished neighbors kept elevated on blocks because they couldn't afford gas to make it run. That left Mish, my three-year-old brother, my little sister Irene, who was five, and baby Béla to watch.

Irene was the problem. Her head was always off somewhere in the clouds. Even worse, she was a wanderer. Today I'd seen her in the field beyond the chicken coop, turned to check on the baby, then swiveled back to find her gone. She'd just fluttered off like a butterfly.

"Anya!" I yelled.

My mother shoved her head out the kitchen door, booting a few cats out, too. "What is it, Pista?"

While we children slid back and forth between languages almost without thinking, Anya and Apa were more comfortable speaking Hungarian at home. Apa didn't want the mother tongue forgotten. *Pista* was Anya's Hungarian nickname for me, even though I never understood how it came from István.

"Irene's disappeared!" I called.

"I'm busy fighting with the stove, son. When your father gets home, he'll expect his supper on the table. You'll have to find her."

Why did Apa have to go off cutting wood? I grumbled to myself. It would be much nicer to have him here at home. Think of all the work we could get done together, like the chicken fence that never seemed to get built.

"Let's go, Mish." I tousled his hair and pulled him from the dirt he was contentedly digging in, then hoisted Béla onto my shoulders. "Irene's lost again."

We trotted past the long chicken coop, then behind the small feed house. Across the empty field beyond, the woods began. The trees were only now beginning to take on spring colors. The tall, slim oak was always the last to find its leaves, Apa said. Apa knew everything. In Hungary, Apa had been a teacher, a respected man. He was still proud, still believed he was special. But in America, if your English wasn't too good, you couldn't teach school. So Apa had become the next best thing—a landowner.

For the next hour or so I ranged over that land, Béla clinging to my hair and ears, Mish scrambling behind, stopping progress to pick bright yellow dandelions for Anya, scrambling some more. Twenty-five acres, Apa claimed it was. An estate in Europe. In South Jersey it was only a few open fields edged with oak and scrub pine, and nothing but swamp beyond.

My sister was sitting beneath one of the pines,

humming to herself and playing with a pile of last winter's cones. Pine needles clung to her dress and stuck out from her long blond braid. There was no use getting angry with her. No use in explaining again that she shouldn't wander off.

"Come on," I said. "It's time to go home."

She looked up, surprised, then grabbed her doll, tucked a few cones in the pocket of her skirt, and followed us back.

Apa was weary when he returned. But still he took the time to brush a strand of hair from Anya's face and graze his lips against her cheek, flushed from the heat of the big black stove. Then he handed her a crumpled dollar bill.

"For the work," he said. "I cut a cord of wood for Mr. Martin today."

Anya carefully smoothed the bill, then hid it in the nearly empty coffee canister. "Can we start credit with this at the store, Mihály?"

"No credit," my father answered automatically, the way he always did. "I will work to support my family, Louisa."

"But surely Mr. Martin would not mind," Anya protested. "He owns the store, too, and gives our neighbors credit. The woodcutting is almost finished. You said so yourself. Our hens are barely over their winter sickness and not laying well. And on its own this dollar will only buy us flour and yeast and lard enough for a week."

My father sat and reached for his chicken soup. "You can always stew another of the old hens. Soon the new chicks will be hatched. In the meantime, I will go to Philadelphia for work. Paul Pelich from over on Eleventh Avenue found work with meatpackers there, and maybe I can, too. I will take the train. Tomorrow."

All of us children gathered around the table watched with big eyes to see what our mother might answer. We knew what it would be. Whatever Apa said was what happened.

"I'll pack some things for you tonight."

"Yes." Apa nodded. He prized obedience highly. "I will take my violin, too. See that István practices on his own in my absence. He needs work on the major scales."

Two times a day, Philadelphia-bound trains of the South Jersey Railroad stopped at our little village— once in the morning, once in the evening. I walked with Apa the mile up the road to the station the next morning. I carried his bag, switching it from one hand to the other as it became heavy. It moved back and forth quite briskly by the time we reached Tuckahoe, the main road, and turned left to follow the tracks, which ran alongside. Apa never noticed. He just strode along, his own hands in his pockets, cap brim pulled over his eyes, violin case slung on a strap across his back, humming slightly to himself.

I didn't mind. Carrying the bag gave me an excuse to follow my father. I liked watching the train come in. The engine was a wonder—all shiny black and steaming. And when the engineer pulled the whistle, he made it sing. Sometimes he even played a little tune with it. That was the best.

We walked the last piece right next to the railroad tracks. Cords of wood were piled in mounds alongside of them.

"Is that your wood, Apa? Cords that you cut?"

Apa broke his stride to consider. "Some of it, yes. For the ironworks up north."

He pulled his hands from his pockets to study the calluses on his palms. "Look, István. In Hungary my hands were never like this. They were smooth as a woman's, with clean nails. In Hungary an educated man is not expected to do physical labor."

"Then why did you leave?"

I thought it was a reasonable question. My father didn't seem so sure. He watched me set down his heavy bag. Finally he decided to answer.

"You are becoming big. But not big enough. You would not understand affairs of the heart, or starting at 'the top of the haystack' . . ."

"What do you mean, 'the top of the haystack'?"

He shrugged. "Your mother had two older, unmarried sisters, and a father who believed they should be married off from the top. I did not agree." Apa almost grinned, then his expression darkened. "The mere thought that someone else might court and win my Louisa while I was working from the top of the haystack . . ." Apa seemed to forget who he was confiding this information to, then suddenly remembered and thrust his hands back out of sight. "And then there was the Great War. All would have been well without the Great War . . ."

"Why?"

"Why?" Apa considered as he began walking again. "Hungary fought on the wrong side, the losing side. In punishment for this, the old Austro-Hungarian Empire was torn to pieces. Hungary lost half of its land, and that land was ravished."

"What do you mean, Apa?"

He grunted. "I mean soldiers stole or destroyed everything they could find. Your mother's family, my family, everyone we left behind, not knowing war was coming—before, we were not rich, but we were comfortable. Afterward . . ."

We'd reached the small station, and I could hear the train coming up the tracks to meet us.

The growing rumble returned Apa's mind to the present, and he relieved me of the bag at last. "You are in charge of the household now, István, the man of the family. Take care of the little ones. Particularly take care of your mother."

I nodded. "How long will you be gone?"

But the train was pulling in, and Apa was jumping aboard.

"As long as it takes!" he shouted back to me over the clangs and puffs. "As long as it takes."

I stood watching the cars and Apa disappear in a cloud of steam. This time the engineer did not play a tune. The train whistle was long and low as it faded into the distance.

Two

"I won't go to school while Apa is away." I made that announcement to my mother at breakfast the morning after he left.

"What do you mean, you won't go to school?" She placed a bowl of hot corn mush before me.

"Apa told me to look after you. He said I was in charge of the family. How can I look after you if I'm at school?"

Anya's lips twitched, but her voice was serious as she sprinkled a little sugar atop my mush with her fingers. A very little. "You want to spend your life in this godforsaken place, Pista? Without an education, that is what you'll do. You will eat your breakfast, and you will go to school. At school you will learn English. Then you will come home and teach *me*."

Sándor looked up from his own bowl. New words interested him if they had a forbidden ring to them. "What's *godforsaken* mean, Anya?"

Anya pulled absently at the hair she'd only just pinned up. "It means there are no relatives and friends, no picnics by the river in the summer. No servants to help." She sighed. "And no mountains."

"Oh." Sándor ducked his fair head back over his breakfast bowl.

"What's a mountain?" Irene asked.

"There, you see," Anya muttered. "My children don't even understand what a mountain is."

Mish stumbled into the kitchen rubbing at his eyes just as Béla's yowls for attention began floating down the stairs. Anya paused, distracted, between the two. I spooned my bowl clean and went to school.

One week passed, then another. We had a letter from Apa, but it contained no money. He had found work in a shoe factory, but learned that it cost more to live in the big city than he had expected. He did not say when he was coming home.

We did nothing but go to school and go to church—always to return to the work. The farm chores just multiplied with Apa away. Anya took care of the morning work with the hens, but she was preoccupied by the eggs she was trying to hatch in the incubator Apa had installed in our cellar. It seemed as if every few minutes she was checking to see if the kerosene lamp was properly heating the water circulating inside the insulated hood that sheltered the eggs. Now in the afternoons I had to feed all six hundred of the molting old hens. They kept right on eating, whether they were laying or not.

Irene liked to drag Mish into the coop and they'd pretend they were collecting eggs. Pretend, because there were few surprise eggs to be found. Still, Irene would bustle between the neat rows of nests Apa had built on either end of the coop. She'd stretch on tiptoes to stick her hand in the hay of the higher ones while Mish poked into the lower ones. Irene always sang away at some song she'd learned in school, with little Mish picking up on a few words here and there. She usually steered clear of the few hens actually sitting in the nests, but one afternoon she grew brave. She thrust her fingers under the dirty-white feathers of a mangy, beady-eyed bird, then let out a squeal. "Pista!"

"Careful of the cluckers!" I yelled from across the room.

"What's a *clucker*?" Irene managed between sucking at her scratched and pecked hand.

I trotted over, hauled out the squawking bird by its legs, and dunked its head in the nearest water pan. "Didn't you listen to the way it clucked to warn you away? It's a chicken that thinks it's hatching its eggs."

She eyed the hen I'd just cooled down. It stalked off, red comb and wattles shaking. "Why can't it hatch its eggs, like Anya is hatching those eggs in the cellar?"

I retrieved the lone egg still nestled in the hay and added it to Irene's wire basket. "Because it's the wrong kind of egg. It's not fertilized."

"Why?"

"Because we have no roosters."

"Why?"

"Because we eat all the roosters when they're still young."

"Why?" This time Mish asked the question.

I began losing my patience with both of them. "Because Apa says they get tough and cranky and bossy and bother the hens when they begin to grow up."

"Just like you." Irene giggled. "Come on, Mish, we have enough eggs."

Snickering like conspirators, they danced out the open door. I winced at the jiggling basket in my sister's hand. She'd probably manage to crack half of the few eggs she'd collected. Before I could give a cranky warning, Sándor made his belated appearance.

He was responsible for cleaning the water pans in the coop, a job he hated. Today he marched directly to the first pan without even a hello. He gingerly swished around the sludge that had settled on the bottom. That was my cue to distract the birds by scattering a pailful of the cracked corn they loved. I bellowed out a *"Here, chick-chick-chick-chick-chick! Here, chick-chick-chick! Come and get it!"*—tossing left and right.

Hens scrambled. It was Sándor's cue to begin his grumbling.

"This water is cruddy!"

"That's why you're changing it. *Here, chick-chick-chick-chick!* Besides, it's a whole lot cleaner than those engines you're always fussing with."

"Ugh." He tossed the water through the open door as I emptied the corn pail. "Engines aren't dirty. They're *greasy*. Grease is thick and smooth and makes things move. Chicken shit is only *chicken shit*."

"Sándor!" I stuck my head out the door to make certain Irene and Mish were gone. "That kind of talk isn't for the little ones. And if Anya heard you—"

"Are you going to tell her?" He moved on to the next pan. "Anyhow"—he smirked—"she probably wouldn't understand the English word. And what exactly do you call *it* when we have to shovel *it* up from under the roosts every weekend?"

"Manure?" I tried. "Manure for the compost pile.

That's what Apa always calls it." I felt on slightly surer ground now.

Sándor sneered. "*Manure.* Won't find me being a farmer when I grow up. I'm going to fix automobiles." He slung more cold water out the door. "Then I'm going to race them, like Barney Oldfield. I'll be the new Speed King of the World!"

"Does Apa know about this?"

Sándor straightened his wiry frame. "When I'm taller than Apa, I can do anything I want!"

That was far more shocking than his earlier words. No one could be brave enough—or foolish enough—to go against the wishes of our father. My ears burned as if Apa himself were listening. I bolted from the coop, sliding on the slimy path Sándor had made by the door. "I'm going to fetch more mash. Since you're not taller than Apa yet, you'd better finish cleaning those pans."

My school was on the other side of the railroad tracks, not too far from the train station. Most days after lessons, I took to walking along the tracks in that direction, maybe trying to put off as long as possible the waiting chores and the arguments with Sándor. I'd walk as far as the station. It had a wide slate roof that jutted from the building almost as far as the tracks. The overhang made a good shelter on rainy days. And I was proud of the sign that hung from the eaves at either end of the building. In big white letters it announced the name of our town for all the train passengers to see: DOROTHY. Somehow that sign made our town real, made me real.

The post office was across the road, right inside Mr. Martin's gray-shingled hodgepodge of a general store. The post office gave me a reason to go in. I could ask Mr. Martin's mother if there was a letter. While she checked, there were a few moments to wander around the store. I liked to smell the cheese, and the vinegar and dill from the big open barrel of pickles. I tried to stay away from the long sausage shapes of the salami and the other meats, though. They always made my stomach rumble, and I was afraid the old lady might hear it.

"Nothing from your father today, Stephen," she usually said.

Stephen. That was my American name, the one

they called me by at school. So many different names to remember. Which one was me?

"Did you hear me, young man?"

"Yes, missus." I made a stiff bow the way my father might. "I thank you."

I left the temptations of the store.

One afternoon I arrived home to find we had company. There was an automobile stopped before the house. Not just any automobile, either. Not a plain old black Model T. This one was long and low and painted a smooth silver that gleamed in the late-day sun. Its top was down, and you could smell the soft leather of its seats half a mile away. You didn't need to be Barney Oldfield or even Sándor to fall for an automobile like that.

I flung my strapped pile of books onto the grass of the front yard and raced for the car. I had one hand out to caress its gleaming beauty—

"Stop!"

I wheeled around.

"Don't touch my Packard! Do you understand English? Don't even think about it!"

My English was coming along just fine. Fine enough that I could have spieled off a few choice phrases I'd learned in the school yard—even more impressive than that word Sándor had used. It was tempting. Especially for the benefit of the man standing on the front porch with my mother. He was dressed in a snappy pin-striped suit. He had spats on his shoes. Pearl gray. His hair was plastered flat with grease, and his eyes were just as oily. It was loathing at first sight.

I never said those words, though, because of Anya. There she stood, Béla in her arms, two children clinging to her skirts, and Sándor staring hungrily at the Packard from behind her back. "Thank goodness." The Hungarian words came out in a rush. "You're home, son. Please explain to this man—"

"Who is he?" I barked.

"The mortgage man. Explain about your father being in Philadelphia. About how there is no money this month to pay. But next month . . ."

I explained, very slowly and clearly, so he could not possibly misunderstand.

The mortgage man snorted. He snorted again, then gave my mother an appraising glance. She looked very young and helpless—and, I suddenly knew, quite pretty. His oily eyes narrowed.

"Tell your mother there are other ways to pay." He tried for a smile, but to me it looked more like a threat. "If she'd like to take a little spin in my Packard—without the kiddies . . ."

I relayed the message. Anya's face turned startled, then bright pink. Her free hand shot out and slapped the mortgage man across his face. His well-fed cheeks swelled in disbelief before he spun on his heels.

"No money next month, you're outta here!" He slammed into his car and ground the engine to life, all six cylinders of it. "Bag and baggage!"

I watched the mortgage man mistreat his fine vehicle around the corner and out of sight. Behind me I heard Sándor's groan of frustration. For once I sympathized with him. Then I dusted from my shirt the spray of dirt left behind. I smiled at my mother, who was still trembling. "You did to him just what I wanted to do, Anya."

Still, I worried about what might happen if Apa didn't get home before next month.

That night I wished for Apa more than ever. Even Sándor was supposed to be in bed, yet, returning from the outhouse, I noticed that the kitchen door to the cellar was open. I slipped down the wooden stairs and followed the dim light past shelves nearly empty of my mother's canned vegetables, all the way to the incubator.

"Anya?" I rushed closer with excitement. "Are the chicks starting to hatch at last? It's been over three weeks, and Apa said it took three weeks—"

Anya was holding a fluffy, limp body in her hand. "I turned the eggs just as your father instructed, Pista. Two times a day, like a mother hen. All three hundred of them. I kept the machine heated with the big kerosene lamp . . ." She stroked the fluff. "They're hatching at last, but something has gone wrong. What did I do?" She gave me a pitiful look. "And what will I tell your father?"

I flopped on the dirt floor and peered under the

cone-shaped canopy of the incubator. There were dead bodies strewn everywhere among the cracked-open shells. I reached in a hand and pulled it back quickly from the heat. "It feels very hot, Anya. Too hot. Did you check the temperature?"

Anya could usually handle any crisis. Now she just sat there with that dead chick in her hand, shaking her head. I scrambled around the circular hood of the machine to squint at the thermometer. "It says 110 degrees, Anya. Apa said it must never go over 103 degrees!" I jerked the rope on its pulley to raise the incubator hood. "If we let in the cool air, maybe we can still save some . . ."

Anya came awake again as we checked each body, searching for signs of life. Soon there were a few dozen chicks staggering around listlessly. We rubbed them, set them down, looked for others. Finally the incubator was in place again, the temperature lowered. We sat back and stared at the disaster—a mountain of tiny, lifeless bodies—then at each other. Anya finally spoke.

"Go to bed, Pista. You have school tomorrow."

"But all these dead chicks——"

"I will take care of them. Only what to tell your father . . . what to tell him?"

I stumbled up the stairs. I didn't know what to say to Apa, either. Surely this was my fault as well as Anya's. I was in charge of the family. I knew what the temperature should have been. How could the heater have made such a mistake? Worse, far worse, what would Apa think when he got home?

The following night I was thrashing about in bed, trying to find a comfortable spot not already taken by Sándor or Mish. That's when I heard the sound through the open window. I stiffened and listened harder. First the chicks. What next?

There were the usual noises of a few night birds, a few insects. There was the barking of the neighbors' mongrels across the dirt road. Their yelps and howls at the moon were regular and barely noticed. Besides, they were kept tied up after dark. No, it was something else. Something creeping around the house. Even my toes tensed. Now it was just below my window, scrabbling under the front porch. I shivered beneath my piece of quilt. It was hard having the care of the household on my shoulders.

Should I waken Anya? She'd been so tired after last night's disaster that she'd barely managed to follow my daily English lesson when supper was done. Then she'd only half smiled and nodded while I made mincemeat of my scales on the violin.

I was the man of the family. I would make up for the hatching mess. I would take care of this matter myself. Besides, it could be a very large raccoon. Or even an opossum. Either would be welcome for the stewpot.

I slipped over my brothers. They hardly stirred.

"A fat possum," I muttered to myself. "A *slow*, fat possum."

I tugged down my nightshirt and journeyed on tiptoe from the small room, through the hall, to the stairs. I took them one at a time, minding the step that creaked. Then it was a matter of getting through the darkened kitchen. The Regulator clock hanging on the wall kept a steady, eerie ticking. Why did it sound so different in the middle of the night?

Finally I was out in the cool air. The moon was full and shone with brilliance over everything. The grass and weeds beneath my bare feet were damp with dew. I stopped to curl my toes in the wetness.

I should have brought a weapon, I suddenly realized. I should have brought the bread knife from the kitchen. But could I go back, retrace all those steps again? Maybe I didn't need the knife.

Then again, did possums bite? I knew raccoons did. I trembled a little beneath the flannel of my long shirt. I decided it would be a possum. Just grab it by the tail, give it a good swing . . . What if it had no tail? What if it was too big to swing?

I didn't like being head of the family. Not at all. I uncurled my toes and finished circling the little clapboard house. I heard the stirring again as I neared the porch. Its sides by the foundation of the house were open, showing the brick support columns. Apa always meant to build a wooden lattice around the opening. Why hadn't he?

I bent to peek into the space and saw something

that shouldn't be there. Heart pounding, I grabbed for it.

A loud *thunk* broke the silence.

Followed by a moan of anguish.

There was something familiar about the pitch of that moan . . .

I dropped the boot in my hands to scramble beneath the porch.

"Apa? Is that you, Apa?"

"*Sssh*. Not so loud, István."

A little light from the moon penetrated even this darkness. I squatted in my nightshirt, watching my father rub his head where he'd cracked it on the low porch floor.

"I thought you were a raccoon," I said inconsequentially. "Or maybe a possum. A fat one."

He rubbed some more. "As you see, that is not the case."

"No."

I waited a little while.

"What are you doing back from Philadelphia, Apa? And why are you under the porch?"

I fancied there was enough light even to see the glare in his eyes. "Why do you think? To protect the house, of course!"

"You could do that easier from *inside*, Apa. And have you been coming home every night since you left?"

"Of course not," he growled. "You think I am an idiot?"

At this point I was unsure what to think, so I didn't answer. Apa noticed.

"I am not an idiot! I only wanted to make certain your mother—all of you—were safe, that you had no unwelcome visitors."

"Who would visit us, Apa? We hardly know anybody. The only visitor we had the entire time you've been away was—"

"Yes?" His head jerked up so quickly, he banged it again.

"—the mortgage man," I finished.

"Hah!" said Apa, forgetting to rub at his new bump. "I never even thought of the mortgage man!"

"I guess not, because you didn't leave us any

money to pay him. And he said he'd take the farm away next month, and kick us out bag and baggage, and Anya had to slap his face, and——"

"Your mother slapped the mortgage man?" A beatific smile crossed my father's face, turning up the ends of his mustache. "She really did?"

I nodded.

"Enough, then." Apa attempted some semblance of decorum within the ridiculously cramped space. "Obviously it is time I returned from Philadelphia. I will do so on the evening train tomorrow."

"But you're already *here*——"

He waved me from his presence. "To bed, son. You have school in the morning and need your sleep. No more will be said of this matter. To *anyone*. Especially not your mother."

"No, sir." I scrambled from under the porch. Then I had a last thought and ducked my head down again. "If you should find a raccoon while you're down there, Apa?"

"What *then*?" His whisper was filled with frustration.

"You could leave it by the back door. For me to find in the morning. I'm sure Anya could figure out how to cook it."

I went back to bed, then remembered I'd forgotten to tell Apa about the incubator accident. Suddenly it didn't seem to matter. I slept easier knowing Apa was on watch under the porch.

THREE

There was no raccoon by the back door in the morning. Apa, however, officially returned from Philadelphia that night, as he'd said he would, pretending to have ridden down on the evening train. He brought a new Sunday dress for Anya, a large string of sausages, and a bag of hard candy for us children. He didn't bring much money, but it was enough for the mortgage.

He also brought the most amazing chandelier. It had arms of brightly polished brass, scores of jangling crystal pendants, and finely etched lamp glasses. He set it atop the empty kitchen table with a flourish.

"But, Mihály . . ." Anya was nearly speechless. "Why such an expensive thing?"

I crept closer to the glorious object. I wanted to touch it almost as badly as the mortgage man's Packard, but I was afraid. I stared up at my father, waiting to learn why he had brought this instead of more food.

"There should be some beauty in life, Louisa," Apa explained. "Look. Crystals from Bohemia!" He tapped one, and it tinkled, pure and clear. "From the old Austro-Hungarian Empire. To remind you of our homeland."

Anya already had a handkerchief to her eyes. "But in this New World, husband, the children need clothing. And food to eat. And we need wire for the fencing. Besides, we have neither gas nor electricity to make it work!" She stopped to sniff and gulp. "And the baby chicks—"

Apa waved his arms dismissively. "There will be no talk of business tonight. The chandelier will look magnificent in the parlor, won't it?"

As if that settled everything, Apa hefted the monster and lugged it into the next room. All of us children followed, even Béla, crawling.

"I will hang it tomorrow," he announced. Then he turned to me. "And tomorrow evening, István, you and I will give a violin concert beneath it. I will play the Haydn piece I've been practicing in Philadelphia, one that he composed for Prince Esterházy in Hungary. You may display your accidentals and triplets."

The unconfessed incubator catastrophe was trial enough on my conscience. Talk of a concert set me near to shaking. In truth, neither my major scales nor my accidentals and triplets had progressed noticeably in my father's absence. I was currently of the opinion that they might *never* progress noticeably. Somehow my father's musical expertise had not descended into the hands of his eldest son. Small wonder those very hands now trembled. Apa noticed.

"You have a fever, son?"

"Maybe, Apa. Maybe I should go to bed."

"Perhaps you should." He glanced past me at the remainder of his brood, already sticky from his gift of sweets. "The rest of you, too. Your mother and I must have some privacy to celebrate my home-coming!"

I spent hours worrying about the concert the next day. I blamed it all on the violin, of course. Specifically the D and G strings, which I could never seem to keep in tune. Terrible screeching sounds floated through my mind all day at school. That meant I had trouble paying attention to the teacher. He was talking about something called *fractions*, and they made no sense to me at all. How could you imagine something to be in pieces? An orange was an orange. An apple was an apple. If you were lucky enough to have either one, you ate it and it was gone. And that was that.

"Stephen Csere!"

I jumped. "Yes, sir, Mr. Strick?"

"You will recite back to me what I've just said."

I broke into a hot sweat and a jumble of Hungarian. My classmates giggled around me, but had the decency to do it behind their hands. First the teacher stared at them. The titters stopped. Then he turned his glare on me.

"Feigning ignorance of the language of our country is not acceptable, young man. Not when we both know that you know better."

I hung my head. The bow of a violin scraped over my brain again, shrieking, leaving my thoughts jangling.

"Stephen?"

"Yes, sir, Mr. Strick?"

"You will understand fractions by tomorrow morning. You will exhibit this understanding on the blackboard for the entire class. Or I will find it necessary to beat the information into you. Is that clear?"

My eyes focused on the long wooden ruler he was slapping onto the palm of his hand. Mr. Strick didn't seem dangerous. He was a slim, smallish sort of man. Yet I *knew* from previous experience that he knew how to make that innocent measuring device into an instrument of torture. I gulped. "It is clear, sir."

The school bell began to ring at that very moment. Its loud clangs meant that it was three o'clock at last. School was over. I was free. I grabbed my books and escaped with my classmates.

I made a space on the kitchen table to finish my homework right after supper. Anya pushed the kerosene lamp closer to make my light better. I smiled my thanks up at her. She smiled back, relaxed. Good. That meant the incubator business had been discussed with my father. Since nothing had been said during the meal, it also meant he'd accepted the accident and the subject was closed. I sighed my own relief, but not too loudly to disturb Apa. He was still in the chair next to me, where he was digesting his dinner with the help of the Hungarian newspapers he'd brought from Philadelphia. I craned my neck to see what he was reading, and caught a fascinating headline about gangsters in Chicago before the pages crinkled and I ducked back to my work. Apa glanced at my notebook.

"So. You are finally working on fractions. I always loved fractions."

My head shot up. "You *did*? Why?"

"Because they are so neat. So precise. Almost as good as decimals."

"Oh." That didn't explain anything to me. I looked at my notes from school again. There weren't nearly enough of them to even begin explaining the mystery. A vision of Mr. Strick and his ruler floated past my eyes. I swallowed hard.

"Maybe you could help, Apa?" He had been a teacher, after all. "Maybe you could explain how a whole number can suddenly become parts of a number? How a whole orange is not whole anymore?"

Apa neatly folded his newspapers. "Hand me that bag, Louisa. The one meant for Sunday."

Anya reached up to a shelf and brought down a paper bag that had missed my detection during the excitement of my father's homecoming. "You will ruin the surprise, Mihály."

"No. For education all is worthwhile."

I watched as Apa opened the bag and carefully pulled out an orange. An *orange*! There hadn't been an orange in the house since last Christmas, and the

Christmas before that. Six more followed, until the bag was empty. Apa smoothed the paper bag and set it aside. Then he lined up the fruit in a row on the table.

"What have we here, son?"

I laughed. "Seven oranges! Even one for Béla!"

"I'm glad to see that your baby arithmetic is still working." He leaned back in his chair. "Now divide them in half for me."

Seriously, precisely, I rolled three oranges to one side, and four to the other. "There. Three plus four makes seven."

Apa frowned. "I asked you to divide them in *half*, István. So they are equal. If we were to share these equally between us at this very moment, how would you feel if I chose to eat four oranges, and left only three for you?"

I swallowed again, this time from thinking about the lovely sweet juice of all those oranges. "It wouldn't be fair! You'd have a whole extra orange!"

"Precisely."

Apa slipped a hand into his pocket and brought

out his penknife. He clicked it open and picked up the fourth orange. Then he began to peel it with his knife. I watched spellbound as he started at the top and worked his blade in circles until the fruit was bare. The spiral of orange skin remaining was absolutely intact, absolutely perfect. He set it down in the center of the table, where it pulsed like a spring.

"Where did you learn how to do that, Apa?"

"From my father."

"Why didn't you ever do that with the Christmas oranges?"

"Because Christmas oranges are always eaten too quickly, too greedily."

"Will you teach me? May I use your knife to try peeling one that way?" Suddenly I desperately wanted to learn his trick.

"No!" He set down the knife. "We are now learning *fractions*!"

He split open the peeled orange down the middle. He placed one piece with each of the sets of oranges. "Tell me again, István. What is half of seven oranges?"

"Why . . ." I stared at the two piles. Something in my head twanged. The bow on the strings of my brain went smooth, then raced into a wild Hungarian dance, a *czardas*. It *was* possible. "It must be three oranges and a half. Add another three oranges and a half and you will have seven!"

Apa cracked a small smile. "That must mean that two halves make one whole. Next we take this open orange, this half." He picked it up. "We count the segments inside."

"Five," I promptly noted. "And five in the other half."

"Would you say, István, that this whole orange is made up of ten segments?"

I considered. "It must be so."

Apa pulled off a segment and popped it into his mouth. I licked my lips as he carefully chewed and swallowed. "Then what fraction of this *whole* orange have I just eaten?"

"One tenth!"

"It is so." Now Apa was truly smiling. "And you shall have another tenth of my Sunday treat."

It was the most delicious fraction of an orange I ever hope to eat.

A few days later I arrived home from school in time to find Apa hauling a big crate into the kitchen.

"What is it, Apa?" I asked.

"It is a present for your mother."

Anya had been watching from her usual spot before the stove. "For me? What—"

"Fertile eggs. Three hundred of them. You will try again."

Anya blanched as Apa relentlessly lugged the crate down the cellar steps.

Four

Spring went fast with Apa back, and soon it was June and I was free from school for an entire, glorious summer. Sándor—to his utter disgust—was promoted to babysitting, and I had all day to spend with my father. And they were long days.

They started at four in the morning, when Apa woke me to teach me how to light the kerosene lamps for the hens in their coop. Our hatchlings had quickly grown from fuzzy chicks to pullets, and would be laying soon, while our old hens were healthy again.

"When the hens are laying, István," Apa explained, "they must eat as much as possible."

"So they can lay more eggs," I verified.

"Even so. They don't mind rising early if there is good mash for them to eat, and clean water to drink."

So Apa demonstrated the correct procedure for lowering the lamps from their spots near the ceiling, checking the wicks and fuel supply, making certain the ropes were tightly knotted after they were raised again. Especially making sure they weren't left too close to a wall or the roof, where their heat might start a fire. Next he reminded me always to crack open the coop windows for a little fresh air. When he was certain I could be trusted with the job, it was Anya who woke me, and I went alone to bring light into the darkness while Apa finished his rest.

I was sleepy, yet it felt good. I was truly helping. I knew Apa was working late every night now at the kitchen table. When the day broke, there were his papers still spread all over it. He was sketching ideas for the farm: new chicken coops, an orchard, special gardens that would be only for growing gooseberries and currants, like those in Hungary. Apa had big plans for our place.

And now with most of the chickens laying eggs at last, there was a little money to spend on these ideas. Twice a week I helped Apa stack wooden crates filled with fresh eggs in his wheelbarrow. Together we pushed the wheelbarrow the mile to the railroad station, where the crates would be loaded into boxcars for the markets in the city.

On days when Apa was feeling very good about things, we walked across the dirt road to the post office and store. There Apa would stop to talk a little with Mr. Martin about business. Every few weeks we would also go to the hotel on the far side of Mr. Martin's. This was owned by the Hellers, and they sold gasoline for cars and kerosene for our lamps.

The Hellers lived in the huge, white-frame building that was part hotel and part meeting place and dance hall for our community. They had six boys, all a little older than me, but it was nice to talk to them anyway. All the boys used to sit on the railing of the big open porch that ran across the front of the building and wait for an automobile to arrive. Then they would fight for whose turn it was to fill the gas tank. How I wished that someday one of them would offer to let *me* do the honors.

That's what I was thinking one hot afternoon in early July. There were the six of them, as alike as peas in a pod, looking big and strong in their overalls and nothing else. They were lined up in a row on the porch railing, legs dangling, drinking soda pop. Charlie and Joe and Fritz and August and Carl and Siggi. I wished I had some soda pop, too.

" 'Lo," I tried.

"How's it going, Steve?"

There it was, *another* name. "Fine, thank you." I dug my boot into the dry sand. A puff of dust rose. It hadn't rained for a while. "I think my father needs some kerosene." I swung the empty five-gallon can in my hand.

Charlie nudged Joe. "Your turn."

Joe swiped at his forehead and glanced at the next brother. "Ah, it's too hot. You can get it, Fritz."

"If it's too hot for you," Fritz allowed, "it's too hot for me."

I stared at them. Usually they argued the other way around. "Maybe," I tried, "maybe I could get it?"

August, perched fourth in line, laughed. He pulled at his overall straps and slipped off the railing. "Nope. It's our job. The stuff's in *our* fuel house. Guess I'll have to get it."

Carl and Siggi suddenly showed signs of life. They tossed away their empty pop bottles. "It was *our* turn!"

Then they were off the porch and scuffling, all trying to get at my can.

Charlie finally bellowed out, "We'll all get it!"

I stepped forward hopefully. I'd only peeked into the fuel house once. I'd barely seen the big tanks in the darkness, but they held unmistakable allure. And that spigot, with the little press pump on the end that you needed only squeeze to get the fuel flowing . . . "I could help, too!"

"Nah." Fritz waved me away. "Go get the money from your pa. Fourteen cents the gallon, like usual."

Spurned again. I turned and shuffled back to Martin's store and my waiting father. "Apa?"

"Yes? What is it, István?"

He was busy studying an equipment catalogue with Mr. Martin. I edged closer for a peek. It was all about generators. Generators! Was Apa thinking about bringing electricity to the farm? No more kerosene lamps to fill and light? No more kerosene lamps to clean?

"Apa, are you going to get—"

My question was never finished. Instead, I was thrown into my father's arms by a tremendous explosion. The entire store rattled and shook. Cans tumbled from shelves; the pickle barrel swayed round and round before toppling into a wave of cucumbers and brine.

There was sudden silence, shattered by another, stronger explosion.

Apa tightened his arms around me for a long moment, then shoved me from his embrace. He and Mr. Martin ran outside. I bolted over the tide of pickles and followed, grinding to a halt at the corner of the store. I stared in disbelief at the sight before me.

The Hellers' fuel house was billowing vast plumes of black smoke into the sky. It was on fire. The wooden hotel next to it was going up in flames, too. But worst of all were the shapes stumbling from the fuel house, alight. Torches brighter than the burning sun.

"*Istenem*," Apa gasped. "*My God*. What has happened?"

My legs crumpled beneath me. I collapsed onto the dirt, hugging my body, shivering through the blast of heat. My father and Mr. Martin ran to help. The helping went on for a long time.

Afterward I could remember none of it.

I opened my eyes the next morning alone in my bed. I squinted through the bright light of day. Why hadn't I been woken to tend to the kerosene lamps for the hens? I threw on my clothes and went down for breakfast. Anya heard me coming and turned from the stove to hug me fiercely. Her eyes were red.

"What is it, Anya?"

"Nothing. Everything. You are alive. Three of those boys are dead. They struck a match because the fuel house was too dark."

I had trouble following the words. "Dead? Who?"

"The Heller boys. Charlie, and August, and Siggi. And the others in the hospital. Promise me you will never strike a match near gasoline, Pista."

I blinked. "I promise, Anya."

"Or near an open can of kerosene, son."

"I promise, Anya." I meant it, too. I sat down, but couldn't eat. If those Heller boys had let me come with them the way I'd wanted . . . I shoved my bowl away. Maybe I would never eat again.

Outside, Sándor saw me coming and raced over. "You saw the fire! The whole thing! Tell me about it! I was stuck here *babysitting*—"

I pushed past him and kept going until I found my father in the big field beyond the feed house. He was bent over a seedling he'd just planted. He must have heard me coming, but he carefully finished patting the little mound of soil around the twig. Then he reached for a bucket of water and poured. Finally he set down the bucket and turned to me.

I opened my mouth in surprise, but no words came. My father's head was bright pink and hairless.

His eyebrows were singed thin, and his mustache, too.

"I have just planted an apricot tree, István." He pointed at other holes he'd dug beyond. The skin on the hand he pointed with was red and raw. "Over there I will plant more. Apple and plum, also. We must bring water every day for the seedlings until they find their roots and grow strong." He studied the frail plant at his feet. "I think maybe we will build a little fence around each one, too, like we did for the garden. To keep the rabbits and deer from eating the seedlings."

"Apa," I finally managed to get out. "Apa. Will your hair grow back? And your mustache?"

He was silent for a long moment. "The mustache, yes. The hair, who knows?" He gazed across his field. "Sooner than those boys will grow back."

I wanted to hug my father as fiercely as Anya had hugged me. Instead, I picked up the empty bucket. "I'll get more water from the well, Apa. We'll have a fine orchard soon."

FIVE

It was a long time before I walked back into town as far as the station and the store and the ruined hotel. I'd follow my father and his wheelbarrow filled with egg crates to where our road met the railroad tracks. Then I'd let my father carry on alone. Sometimes I'd balance on the shining silver rails waiting for Apa's return. Sometimes I'd just turn around and head back home. The woods to either side of the dirt road seemed very thick and dark then. I would not look into them. But once in a while I would bend down to pick up a stone and throw it with all my might into the darkness. The stone was for all those Heller boys. They were, and now they were not.

Afterward, I would run.

"I made *kalács*, Pista," Anya said. "The way you like it, with lots of *lekvár*." She sliced the pastry on the table in front of my place.

"Thank you, Anya." But I could hardly eat the piece of cake she handed me, even though its layers of jam were extra thick. I shoved bits of it around, then looked up to see my mother giving my father a worried glance over my head.

"Who needs cake?" Apa growled from deep down in his throat. He turned to Sándor, sitting on his other side, and ruffled his lank, fair hair. "You don't, do you?"

Sándor's mouth was very full. He shook his head violently and dove for another slice. Apa stared farther down the table at Béla in his high chair. His tiny fingers were busily digging out the jam. Some of it got to his mouth, but most of it was spread over his cheeks and forehead. "Béla does not need cake!" Apa roared. "Wild Indians in war paint never need cake!" Béla giggled at the attention. He stuck two fingers in his mouth, then aimed them at the layers of jam again.

Apa's eyes slid past Mish, head bent over his plate, cramming the dessert very fast, as if it might suddenly disappear. They stopped on Irene. "My daughter certainly doesn't need cake!"

My sister answered very decisively. "Yes, I do, Apa. And so does my dolly." She picked up her spoon and fed a crumb to the doll cradled in her left arm.

Apa's eyebrows rose. He finished circling the table with his glance, then pushed back his chair. "Well, *men* don't need cake." He reached for another slice and strode to the door. "Let's get moving, István. We *men* have work to do this afternoon."

Sándor swallowed quickly. "When will *I* get to be a man, too, Apa? I'm fed up with babysitting. I never get to do anything interesting, like Pista. I never get to do anything I *want* to do anymore!"

"You are now going through the same apprenticeship as your brother, Sándor. When *you* are ten, you may join us."

Sándor scowled. It wasn't the answer he wanted to hear. I picked up my *kalács* and proudly followed Apa.

"What are we going to do, Apa?" I rubbed jam-sticky fingers on my pants and went through the feed house door behind my father.

"We are going to cut some of that rye I planted for the hens. But first we must sharpen the scythes."

"May I help?"

Apa motioned me toward his grinding wheel standing next to one wall. "Sit on the stool, István. *You* are going to do the sharpening."

I watched my father inspect the first scythe. He picked up a hand stone and stroked the half circle of the blade again and again. He raised the blade like a sword to light streaming from the window. "The edge becomes too thick." He walked over to his anvil and placed the blade flat, then peened the edges with blows of a hammer.

All this time I sat on the stool, watching and waiting. When would it be my turn?

Apa finally handed me the scythe. "Pedal the wheel stone with your foot, István. Smooth the rough edges."

I worked my feet very hard then, until the wheel spun fast. I moved the scythe close—

"Mind your eyes, son."

I nodded, and set the blade to the turning stone. Sparks flew. I squinted my eyes, making them very narrow, and pedaled harder. It was wonderful watching the blunt edge turn smooth and sharp.

"Enough," Apa finally said. "Leave a little blade to cut grass with!"

I grinned and let up on the pedal. Then Apa handed me the second, smaller scythe. "What?" I asked.

"Use the stone," he said. "If it needs more, use the hammer and anvil."

After much smoothing with the stone, I know I pounded that blade more out of shape than in, but Apa didn't stop me. It felt so good to test my strength against the big hammer and the hard anvil. I pounded for a long, long time. Only then did I feel Apa's hand on my shoulder.

"I think it's sharp enough, son. Let's go cut some rye."

We worked in the field under the hot sun. I sweated next to my father, bending from the waist for each stroke the way he did, cutting a path through the grass. We stopped only to pull off our shirts and drink from a water jug until the sun began to go down. Then I straightened my aching back and turned to admire all the rye we'd cut. I felt very tired, but very grownup.

Apa pulled the hand stone from his pocket and stroked his blade thoughtfully as he, too, surveyed his domain, far across the field and road to the neighbors' place, then back to the woods behind us. "I think next year we'll need a bigger field, István. We'll grow more rye for the hens, and some corn for them, too."

"Yes," I answered. "They love corn."

He stroked again and I noticed for the first time

that his mustache had grown back to its usual magnificence. His eyebrows were bushy again, too. The top of his head was no longer pink. In fact, it had a soft, dark down sprouting on it.

"So we'll have to clear more trees," Apa continued. "A little each day."

"I'll sharpen the axes, Apa," I piped up proudly. "Now I know how."

"Indeed." A twinkle came into his eyes. "And I will buy some dynamite."

"Dynamite?" I stiffened.

Apa grinned. "For the stumps. There's nothing as satisfying as removing stumps with dynamite."

Why had my stomach suddenly gone queasy on me? "But the neighbors hook up horses to the stumps with tackle, and let the animals do the work."

"Do you notice any horses in our field, István?" He didn't wait for my answer. "Besides, this is the modern age and we must move into it with modern methods."

I stared at the waiting woods. "Will there be fire?"

"No fire. You'll see."

I manfully tried to shrug off my doubts. Apa was rarely wrong. We gathered our shirts, shouldered our scythes, and walked home across the field.

Somehow the neighbors got wind of Apa's unusual stump-clearing plans. In fact, most of the town did. Perhaps it was because he ordered the dynamite at Mr. Martin's store. Anya got wind of it, too. She shook her head on the Saturday morning in August that had been set aside for the operation.

"You think this is wise, Mihály?" Anya clattered a pan on the stove much more loudly than usual. "And surely you won't take the boy!"

I probably wasn't supposed to hear this, but I'd just been rounding the doorway from the hall. I stopped short and kept from sight.

"I'm doing this for the boy, Louisa. Fire must be fought with fire, one explosion with another. He can't walk in fear the remainder of his life."

"Even yet . . . please reconsider, husband."

Anya never challenged Apa. I couldn't let my father become angry with her. I squared my shoulders and sauntered into the kitchen. "It's a perfect morning, isn't it, Apa? You said there should be no wind, and there isn't any. Not a puff."

Anya sighed and clanked the coffeepot. Apa slapped my back. "It's just as we ordered."

Everything was prepared. We'd chopped down the trees day by day. We'd cut through the ring of roots around each trunk. Next to each stump was a small hole we'd dug, empty and waiting. Apa picked up his parcel of dynamite from the feed house and strode across the field toward the woods, which were smaller now.

I followed him, suddenly noticing several automobiles pulled to the side of the two roads that squared off our property. Behind the mud-splattered Model T's stood a disreputable-looking truck. Behind that was a horse and wagon. A knot of men gathered at the end of our field. Apa nodded at them formally and carried on.

We reached the first stump. Apa pulled out a short stick of dynamite, thinner than his smallest finger. He carefully placed it in the waiting hole, and attached a fuse line. I backed off a pace or two and watched him gingerly cover the stick with soil. Finally, Apa lifted his head from his labors.

"Move, István. All the way back to the road where Mr. Martin and the other neighbors are."

I considered. I hadn't been sleeping well for too long. When night came, fiery blasts seemed to keep running through my head. Over and over they came, all the time. I was no coward, but obviously needed to prove it—and just watching this explosion from a distance would prove nothing. I shoved my hands behind my back so my father couldn't see the unexplainable trembling in them.

"I'll wait with you, Apa."

"You will move when I say!" he barked.

I moved. In fact, I ran like a rabbit. When I reached the road, I turned to see Apa strike a match and bend over his fuse. Then *he* ran. Like a deer.

When it came, the explosion was stupendous. I pulled my arms from my head and struggled from my knees, where I mysteriously found myself. I did all this in time to see chips of wood and dirt flying everywhere. But there was no fire.

The men around me shuffled their feet and blew out their breaths. I did, too. Then they began to yell.

"Nice work, Mike!"

"All right if we take a look at how you set up the next stump?"

Across the field, Apa brushed pine chips from his shirt proudly. "Yes, of course."

The crowd flowed from the road. At the rear of it sauntered Sándor. "Where did you come from?" I asked.

He grinned at me. "From behind old man Marsh's Model T. You think I was going to miss this, just because I'm still eight?"

So together we followed the crowd, arms swinging by our sides. When I glanced down at my hands, they were no longer trembling. I pushed past the neighbors' long legs and arrived first.

"It was wonderful, Apa! May I light the next fuse? Please?"

Apa smiled down on me. "No, István. Maybe next year, though, when you're just a little older."

S I X

Anya was homesick. This startling fact revealed itself one evening during supper. She'd served everyone, then ignored her own food to sit staring through the screen door at the vista of the well, the outhouse, the chicken coop.

"What is the trouble, Luzzika?" Apa took another bite, then smiled with pleasure. "Your noodles are delicious. *Nagyon finom.*"

They were, too. Anya had been rolling, cutting, and pinching dough all through the sweltering August afternoon. Then she boiled it and mixed it with soft curd cheese and sugar. I ate the dish as if I'd never get enough. My brothers and sister did, too. Only Anya wasn't touching her food. Instead she rearranged damp locks of hair around her face.

"I've tried, Mihály," Anya murmured. "So hard. But sometimes I miss my family. I miss our old country."

"Pah," Apa declared. "The fullness of summer is no time for such thoughts. Your homesickness will pass."

Anya did not appear convinced of that. The rest of us were curious.

"How can Anya be homesick when she's already here at home?" Irene wanted to know.

"It is because she has two homes," Apa replied. "The home of her heart, here with us, and the home of her childhood, back in Hungary. When you children grow up, you may miss your parents, too."

Irene considered. "Then I will come and visit you and Anya," she declared. "And I'll bring my children."

Mish squirmed from his chair and ran to hug Anya. "Don't be sad," he said. "I'll never go away at all. Then you can't get homesick for me!"

Anya smiled and kissed Mish. But still she didn't eat.

Apa noticed. "Very well, then," he announced. "What we need is something different. We need a mountain and a river and an event—perhaps a picnic. The mountain and river we must imagine, but the picnic can be arranged, I think."

"A picnic? When?" I shouted it out, but I wasn't the only one. The clamor was so great that even baby Béla began pounding on his high chair in excitement.

"Hush, all of you," Apa ordered. "Calm yourselves. The picnic will be sooner rather than later. And you, dear heart"—Apa nodded across the table—"will be the guest of honor." He glanced out the door to the evening sky. He studied the sunset's edges of purple and orange. "Why not tomorrow afternoon? I think the day will be fine."

Anya perked up. "If it is to be a picnic, and if I am to be the guest of honor, then I shall expect my servants to prepare it for me."

"Yes!" I cried out. "Oh, yes. We'll do everything. Won't we, Sándor? Won't we, Apa?"

Apa gave me a mock frown. "A servant's job is not an easy one. Are you sure you are able, István?"

"I'm quite sure." And I was. I looked across the table to Anya. Now she was laughing. She picked up her fork and began to eat.

It was a beautiful day. The sun was bright, the sky was blue, with just a few puffy white clouds floating through it. But it became hotter and hotter as the morning wore on. Maybe that was because I'd been working at the stove boiling eggs for our picnic.

Everyone but Béla and Anya had gathered around Apa last night to work out the menu. We decided that simple might be best. We would pack some of Anya's bread along with cheese and hard sausage. And the eggs. Now I left the stove for the table, where I poured a small pile of salt onto a half sheet of old newspaper, gathered the sides, then carefully twisted the edges together. Irene was kneeling on a chair across from me, humming as usual, fastidiously packing a basket with tablecloth and napkins. Sándor and Mish were in the yard picking ripe peaches from our oldest fruit tree. Apa had walked to Mr. Martin's store to purchase a special bottle of wine.

"A picnic would not be a picnic without a proper bottle of wine," he'd declared.

"Will I get to taste it?" I asked.

"Me too!" Sándor yelled.

Apa raised his eyebrows. "Not you too. Neither of you, in point of fact. Wine is for very special occasions only, and for adults only."

Anya fixed her hair and put on her summer church dress. Apa wore his good shirt and tie, but decided that because of the heat his suit jacket would not be required. I oversaw the scrubbing of hands and faces of all the younger ones—at no little danger to myself. I was pumping the well handle, after all.

Irene held Béla nearby and dabbed a little moisture on him. Then she very delicately did the same for herself. Sándor pushed Mish under the cold stream till he screamed bloody murder. I kept pumping. Then Sándor cupped his hands under the water, as if to deal with himself. I noticed the wicked gleam in his eye too late. In a moment the stream was squirting at me—full in the face! All down my neck and shirt! I gave the pump a final shove and dove for the water to return the favor. Only Apa's timely appearance prevented full-scale war.

But at last we were marching by the chicken coop, across our field, past the craters of recently exploded stumps, out of the scorching sun, and into the coolness of the woods beyond. Even a few of the cats padded after us in curiosity. It was quite a parade.

Apa was in the lead, of course. He threaded between oak and pine, carefully sheltering his violin case from the scratches of outstretched branches.

"This is better than Transylvania," he called back. "Far better. Here there are no gamekeepers. We make our own path through virgin wilderness."

Behind me, Sándor let out a bloodcurdling cry. Anya, her arms full of a wriggling Béla, spun in alarm. Sándor laughed. "I'm an Indian!"

Mish shouted, "Me too!" and tried a few whoops.

Irene clutched her doll. "Quiet! I am an Indian lady, and you're waking my baby!"

Apa forged on. He called a halt in a small glade where the sun broke through to linger over several fallen tree trunks. He turned to Anya. "Will this do, dear heart? Look . . ." He gestured toward the cluster of scrubby pine trees ahead. "Only there the great mountain begins. It rises very high, but if you lean back you will see that the last of the winter's snow still glistens upon its peak." He smiled. "And if you listen very hard, you will hear the river rushing through the valley just beyond. This is obviously the last flat place upon which to spread our picnic feast. The last place where huge, dangerous boulders may not rain down upon our heads."

I found myself searching for the dangerous boulders Apa described. There was only a thick covering of fallen pine needles, brown and slick beneath our feet. Anya, looking quite hot and ready to put down the baby, nodded in relief. Mish trotted up with the blanket he was carrying. "I'm hungry. When do we get to eat our picnic?"

We spread the blanket on the bed of pine needles, arranged ourselves around the picnic baskets, and ate. Then the good part began. Apa removed his violin from its case and set it ready to hand. Next he pulled the cork from his bottle of wine and carefully poured two glasses. He handed one to Anya. His own he held high before her.

"A toast is called for. To your health and happiness, my dearest one. *Egészségére.*"

He touched his glass to hers with a little clink, then took a sip. With a smile, Anya did the same. We children only stared. We had never seen this ritual before. Then Apa raised his glass again. This time he raised it to the rest of us.

"To the children of my heart. May they grow into everything I wish for them."

He downed the wine. With a flourish, he picked up his violin. He began to play. But it was not the usual music that he played. Oh, no. Not Haydn or Beethoven or Bach. This was different. This was special.

I lay back on the blanket and closed my eyes so I could listen better. It was beautiful music. It was sad music, and happy, and everything in between. It swooped and soared like the birds, then changed into the wind through the trees, the wildness of the woods. It sounded like laughing and crying. It sounded more marvelous than anything I had ever heard in my life. It carried me with it as it went on and on. I never wanted it to stop. When it did, I opened my eyes. There were tears in Anya's.

"Apa," I asked. "Apa. Where did that music come from?" If I could play music like that someday—if only for a few precious moments—I would practice the violin forever.

Apa was gazing at Anya. "From the soul, István. From the very soul of our old country."

Anya wiped her eyes and drank from her glass again. "Your father is *Csángo*, children. His clan is all a little crazy. Sometimes I think they have a touch of Gypsy in them, too."

Apa's eyes gleamed as he refilled my mother's glass. "Have another sip, Louisa, and I will play for you till eternity."

Sándor made a rude noise. "Silly stuff," he muttered.

"No," Irene protested. "Lovely stuff. Tell us a story about the music, Apa. A story about Hungary."

Apa played a few more notes on his instrument, then set it aside. "Perhaps I will. But it must be a good story." He loosened his tie and rolled up his sleeves while he thought. "Perhaps I will tell the story of how you children came to be named. There's some music in that, some poetry and history, too. Maybe you are old enough to understand."

Sándor stretched for a peach and bit into it. Béla curled up in Anya's lap and began drifting off to sleep. Irene snuggled as close to Apa as she could. Mish set himself between my legs. I brushed a few ants from his shirt and waited.

Apa nodded at me. "We begin with István."

"Why always István?" Sándor grumbled.

"Because he is the eldest. That is the way life works." And Apa began.

"Once upon a time—more than a thousand years ago—Hungary was as wild as America. But it was a different kind of wildness, a vast plain spread between the great mountains to the east and those to the west, always mostly flat—"

"Flat like South Jersey?" I interrupted.

"Yes." He nodded. "But with rich earth, rich and

black between its rivers, not like the sandy soil of this place. It was good earth in which to grow things, and when the wild hordes swept down from the East on their strong little ponies, following the fabled stag they hunted, one tribe decided to stay. It was the Magyars. After a time a great leader rose among these people. He brought civilization and Christianity to the Magyars. He was a noble and wise man, and his name was István. This István became first king, then saint. Our István is named after the great King István of Hungary." Apa paused. "And also after my own father."

I was sitting very straight by this time. A king! A king and a saint, both. Not to mention a grandfather. This was a very fine name I had been given. With a name like this it didn't matter how people chose to translate it. "Thank you, Apa."

Sándor pouted. "It's not fair. I'll never catch up with Pista."

"But you have, and a little more, besides. You're already taller than your brother is," Apa said with a laugh. "Besides, your name is also wonderful, because I named you after Sándor Petőfi, a great poet."

"A poet!" Sándor scoffed.

"Wait. Let me finish." Apa smiled at Anya. "You see how curious life is, Louisa. The poetry doesn't seem to be taking, but the questioning, protesting nature is already in place." He twisted his head back to my brother. "Petőfi was something besides a poet. He was a leader in the great revolution of 1848. He led the country against our Austrian oppressors—"

"He was a soldier?" Sándor broke in.

"Yes. He fell in battle for Hungary's independence, but his poems and songs still live on, still rouse the people." Apa threw back his head and recited with great passion:

> *Stand up, Magyars, your country calls!*
> *Now is the time, or not at all!*
> *Are we to live as slaves or free?*
> *Choose one! This is our destiny!*
> *By the God of all the Magyars,*
> *we now swear,*
> *we swear never again the chains*
> *to bear!*

The sword shines brighter than the chain,
shows the arm off hard and plain,
and yet we still wear chains in shame!
Give us the sword in our fathers' name!
By the God of all the Magyars
we now swear,
we swear never again the chains
to bear!

"Wow. 'The sword shines brighter than the chain.' "
Sándor's gray eyes gleamed like steel. "That's not
bad. Not bad at all."

Apa nodded his head in agreement, and looked
ready to launch back into the poem, but Irene was
pulling at him. "Me! I'm next, Apa."

Apa gently tugged her blond braid. "So you are.
But your mother had your naming. You came right
after the Great War, and your name means *peace*."

Anya smiled on my sister. "It was also the name
of your grandmother and great-grandmother both.
Two good, strong women."

Irene skipped right past the *peace* business. "Both?

Isn't it lucky, then, that my dolly has the very same name." My sister cuddled back against Apa, satisfied.

Mish yawned. "Where did I come from, Apa?"

Apa laughed. "You came from heaven, just like your brothers and sister. As to your name—Mihály—that came from me, little one."

"Good." He made a pillow of my legs and closed his eyes.

"That only leaves Béla," I pointed out. "What about him?"

Apa glanced at the sleeping baby. "He is the musical part of my story. Béla is named for Béla Bartók, the greatest of today's Hungarian composers." He picked up his violin. "Bartók writes modern music, complicated music, from the brain. But also he writes lullabies for children, from the heart." Apa played again. This time the music was soft and soothing. It slipped right beneath the heat's heaviness, and I found myself leaning back on the blanket again, my eyes closing, too.

An ominous rumble woke me. I sat up and rubbed my eyes. Anya was already stuffing leftovers into the picnic baskets. Apa was thrusting his violin into its case.

"István." He saw I was awake. "A storm comes. Collect the others. They play these Indians and Cowboys somewhere."

"Cowboys and Indians," I murmured. Luckily, he was too busy to hear me.

"Quickly!"

I did it quickly, but they weren't playing Cowboys and Indians when I found them. Instead, Sándor had a stick raised like a sword over a kneeling Irene. He was shouting over the rising storm, "Are you a slave or free?"

"Free!" She thrust her doll forward. "Look! We have no chains!"

"Then swear!" he bellowed.

I grabbed Irene with one hand and a mystified Mish with the other. The sky was already black around us. "Save your swearing. A storm is coming!"

Too quickly it arrived. Wind rose from nowhere, bending the trees around us. Hard, cold rain began to fall as we raced back to the glade. Worse was the lightning. It slashed across the forest like a thousand gunshots at once. The first crack froze us all in our places at the edge of the clearing. The second set us in motion.

"Louisa!" Apa handed Anya the violin case, took the baby. I struggled with the largest of the baskets. Sándor was doing his best with the other. Mish had already dropped the blanket that was his responsibility, while Irene was valiantly trying to protect her doll.

"Leave the picnic things," Apa ordered. "We will find them tomorrow. Now we will run for home."

We ran, but the lightning seemed to follow us. It bolted over our heads, almost atop the crashing thunder. I felt the hair on my arms rise. My body was charged. Charged like Apa's music, charged like the poem. Charged with electricity like heathen hordes sweeping over the plains.

"Move, István!"

Apa was behind me, shepherding me and the others around and past countless trees. Such endless woods! Would we never find our home field? Another crack of sharp, cutting brightness came. On its heels, the sky roared yet again. Then the trees broke open. I raced across the field, spreading my arms to the rain. And there was our farm, our house.

Once we were safely gathered, shivering in the shelter of the kitchen, once Anya had counted heads to be certain we were all there, I could let out the feeling still inside me. The electricity.

"That was some picnic!"

Anya set down the violin case to wring water from her hair, which had fallen loosely over her shoulders. "Yes, it was. But we didn't have storms like this in Hungary, Mihály."

"No," Apa agreed. He hugged Béla to his chest as he stared out into the tempest. "Isn't our new country magnificent?"

SEVEN

That autumn I became the proud owner of a BB gun. It certainly never would have happened if we hadn't been attacked by what my father called *vermin*, but what I called a blessing in disguise.

Those trees we'd chopped down to make the field bigger for planting were now neatly cut and stacked in cords next to the feed house. The wood was seasoning, Apa said. When he considered it sufficiently seasoned, armloads would be carted into the kitchen for Anya and the stove. It was quite a lot of wood, piled in an impressive mound. My sister and brothers had already found the woodpile irresistible as a hiding place. Apa didn't approve. Anya became absolutely fanatical on the subject.

"You children will *not* play in the woodpile!" she reminded them each morning. "Not today, and not tomorrow. In fact, never!"

"But, Anya," Sándor complained. "I have to do something with the little ones while I'm babysitting. It's so perfect for our games—"

"And will it be perfect when it comes tumbling onto your heads? When Mish or Irene or Béla is injured—or worse?"

"You're treating us *all* like babies, Anya." Sándor wouldn't let it go.

"You are babies!"

"Not me!" Sándor stretched his long, skinny body. He'd grown more since summer and was now not merely taller than me but upsettingly taller than me. "I'm in the third grade at school, and nine years old since last week!"

"So then you are quite big enough to understand what I'm saying," Anya replied. "And to obey me."

That shut my brother up for a while. But the

woodpile was still irresistible—to other creatures, as well. Peeking through its gaps, I noticed nests of field mice setting up housekeeping for the coming winter. They looked so busy and pleased with themselves that I let them be and said nothing about them, not even to my father. Which never mattered anyway, because it was bigger game that came to be a problem.

It happened on one of the first really crisp nights of the season. I'd been pushed to the edge of the bed by my younger brothers and was lying there becoming colder and colder. I considered my choices for correcting the situation.

I could grab the end of the quilt and give it a mighty yank. Then it might actually become long enough to cover my freezing toes. Unfortunately, that would also wake the boys, and there'd be some biting and scratching before they resettled themselves—with just as much of the covering as before. They didn't like their sleep disturbed.

Or I could get up and run very fast to Anya's cedar chest in the hallway. Once there, I could pull out another quilt, the winter one she hadn't yet aired for the season. That was the puffy feather bed that I truly loved, the one Anya had brought all the way from Hungary. But it would smell of mothballs. I squirmed in indecision. Sándor pounded my back, twice.

Then again, I could get up and just close the window. But Apa believed in open windows in nearly all weather. "It's good for the lungs," he always said. "And it makes you sleep more deeply, too."

I hadn't yet figured out how you could sleep deeply when the cold was keeping you awake. So I pondered this mystery for another little while. I was reaching for my feet in the hope of rubbing some warmth into them when the first squawk sounded through the night. My body went rigid. After a long moment, another squawk followed. This one was not merely outraged. This one curdled the blood.

I slid from bed and onto the cold floorboards. The same instant I heard Apa banging from the bedroom down the hall. Sándor merely rolled over into my spot on the mattress. I gave my brother a shove out of principle, then chased after my father. By the time I found him in the kitchen, he was already lighting a lantern.

"What's happening, Apa?"

"Something's after the chickens."

"A raccoon?"

"Raccoons don't eat chickens. At least, not alive. They aren't cold-blooded hunters."

"Oh. It couldn't be a rabbit or a deer then, either, because—"

But Apa had already rushed through the door. By the time I caught up with him, he was inside the chicken coop. I wasn't anxious to follow in my bare feet, so I just stood outside, shivering and watching his lamplight bob around the long room.

Then I heard the low growl. It wasn't anything like Apa's make-believe growls. This growl was wild and threatening. My spine tingled as the sound was repeated. Other noises were coming from the coop now, too. It was the hens on their roosts, fussing over their disturbed rest. But mostly it was Apa, yelling and whooping. The next thing you knew, a long, sleek, furry thing raced right out the door of the coop. It stopped short for just an instant when it saw me—enough time for its yellow eyes to catch mine. They looked just like the mortgage man's. For a heart-stopping moment we glared at each other before it was slithering off again, busy hanging on to the hen gripped in its jaws.

"Apa! It's here! It's—" Too late. "It's gone."

"Which way did it go, István?"

The light of the lantern caught me in the face, blinding me for a second. I finally pointed off toward the field. "That way, I think."

"Never mind." Apa was staring at the ground. "We need only follow this trail of feathers."

We did, and they landed us squarely before the woodpile. My father stood there holding the lantern, watching its light shine on the spattered drops of blood that belonged to his hen.

"What was it, Apa?"

"A weasel." He sighed. "And now that he's found our coop and tasted first blood, he'll be back."

I covered one bare foot with the other, trying to warm both. "What will we do?"

"Nothing more tonight." Apa turned toward the

house. "But tomorrow we will go to Mr. Martin's store and buy a gun."

I was sure morning would never arrive. This time it was not the cold bedroom that kept me awake. It was the thought of going with my father to buy a gun. Visions of target practice and hunting and other delights filled my head. What *couldn't* Apa and I do with a gun!

Anya did not have to wake me at four to light the lamps for the hens. I was already slipping into my clothes when she tiptoed into the room. And after the chore was done, I couldn't fall back to sleep for a few hours the way I usually did. Where was the sun? Why was it hiding this morning of all mornings?

When I finally presented myself for breakfast, rumpled and bleary, Anya was still stoking the stove.

"You're up early, Pista." She smiled at me. "Is school going to be so exciting today?"

"School?" I wailed. "School? But I can't possibly go to school today! Apa and I must go for a gun! To catch the weasel in the woodpile!"

Anya handed me a cup filled with warm milk and

just a dash of coffee, for flavor. I stared at the frothy pale bubbles with dismay. "If I go to school, the buying will be done before I'm out. I'll miss everything!"

Apa strode into the kitchen just then, smoothing his mustache. He put an arm around my mother and gave her forehead a kiss. "Good morning, dear heart." Anya smiled. Only then did my father turn to me. "What is this you're planning to miss, István?"

I opened my mouth to renew my outrage, but Anya intervened. "He claims you promised to buy a gun today, Mihály." She paused, her smile fading. "You know how I feel about guns."

"How *do* you feel about guns, Anya?" I asked.

"Hush, son," Apa said. "Remember your mother's father and brother were killed in the Great War."

"But that was far away in Hungary," I protested. "After you'd safely come to America. They could have come, too, couldn't they?"

"István!" Apa warned.

Stubbornly I forged ahead. "Nobody made them stay. And how do you know it was from guns that they died?"

"*Russian* guns," Anya clarified.

"Hah!" I countered. "This will be an *American* gun! And anyway, it's not *people* Apa and I are after, it's that nasty, vicious weasel who's going to eat all our hens if we don't do something about him. You should have seen his eyes, Anya. If you'd seen his eyes for just one second, you'd know——"

Apa put his hand on my shoulder to still my tongue.

"Why don't I meet you at school, István. After classes are finished. Then we'll go to look at the wares in Mr. Martin's store. We will look and consider most carefully."

I stared at my father, then my mother. Normally I'd feel bad when I knew Anya was about to lose another battle. Not this time. I thrust my nose into my frothy milk so she couldn't see the grin spreading across my face.

Apa was waiting outside the school at three o'clock, just as he'd promised. I'd had an awfully hard time concentrating on my classes again. It was lucky we hadn't started anything new and tricky today, like those fractions.

"*Szervusz*, Apa!" I joyfully greeted him.

"Hello, son."

We set off along the railroad tracks toward the store. Apa stuffed his hands in his pockets. "You had a good day at school?"

I nodded, concentrating on jumping from tie to tie without touching the gravel or weeds between. "It was all right."

"So." He strode from the ties to the gravel embankment and strolled another little bit. "My day was all right, too, more or less. Although I had to compromise some in the course of it." He whistled a few bars almost tonelessly.

"Compromise?" My foot slipped onto the forbidden gravel. I wasn't sure I liked the sound of the word. "What does that mean?"

"It means your brother and sister got out of school before you did. I had to promise to bring them sticks of candy so they'd go straight home."

I nodded. That was only fair, since they'd be missing the best part at the store. "Is that all it means?"

"Well, I also had to do a little compromising with your mother. Sometimes it is necessary to compromise with women. Especially on the smaller battles, so the larger ones can be won."

That sounded more serious. "I'm not sure I understand . . ."

Apa stopped several yards from me. I stopped, too.

"Walk toward me, son. Just one step."

Mystified, I jumped off the tracks to do as he bid. My father walked one step toward me.

"Now take another step."

I did. So did he. We faced each other.

"That is compromise, son. We both take a small step, we both give up a little ground."

I shook my head, still confused.

Apa smiled. "Now imagine it is your mother stepping toward me, instead of you. She gives up a little territory and . . ." He paused and looked at me.

Light began to dawn. "Does this mean we don't get a gun, Apa?"

His smile turned broader. "No. It merely means we do not get a very *dangerous* gun."

And that is why Apa and I came back with a BB gun.

It was sufficient for a weasel, Apa claimed. For myself, I didn't mind too much having to ignore all of Mr. Martin's .22 rifles. *Our* BB gun looked almost the same, after all. *Ours* was a superior type, not one of those hand-lever Daisys. It was a Benjamin with a compressed air chamber. It had a piston rod in front, and it was necessary to pump it up before use. Its wooden stock was brightly polished, its barrel was shiny black. It was truly a thing of beauty. On top of which, I was allowed to carry it all the way home.

EIGHT

We did not catch the weasel immediately. First it was necessary to practice with our new weapon. For this purpose Apa and I made our own private excursion into the wilderness—much, much farther than the territory we'd explored during Anya's picnic.

"Training and distance are both essential for safety," Apa said. "We will go on Saturday morning."

Although Saturday was only two days away, I was convinced this was an eternity. School once more became an agony. I survived this time only by drawing wicked weasels all over the margins of my notebook. Curiously, the weasels' slinky bodies became increasingly thinner and thinner, their eyes larger and larger. At last, these creatures were nothing but eyes: huge devious voids into which I felt I could easily slip and drown. My newfound artistic talents were a wonder, yet the greatest wonder was that Mr. Strick never noticed any of this.

But Saturday did come. Anya packed a lunch for my father and me at dawn, not with great enthusiasm.

"Come now, Louisa." Apa placed a finger teasingly beneath Anya's chin, lifting her head for a quick kiss. "Spare a smile for your mighty hunters. We might even return with game for the supper pot."

"Wild boar?" Anya asked.

Apa laughed. "More likely squirrel. We're heading for the Jersey swamps, not for the Carpathian Mountains surrounding your father's hunting lodge."

"Wild boar I truly wouldn't mind," Anya said.

"I know, dear heart, but those days—the days of the great hunt against a worthy adversary—they are gone forever."

"Not the hunt itself, but the *feeling* . . . why did that have to end, Mihály?"

I wasn't certain what my mother was really asking. Was she getting homesick again? The question made Apa's laughter disappear. "You know I cannot answer that. I only know that times change, and we must do our best to survive with them." He threw the lunch into his knapsack, added a bottle filled with water, slung the gun over his shoulder, and turned to me. "Let's go, István, before Sándor wakes and begs to join us. It becomes harder and harder to refuse him, but in this case he really is too young."

Apa paused a moment longer by the door. "I nearly forgot, Louisa. I hired the Marsh boy from Thirteenth Avenue to tend to the hens today, so you could have a little holiday, too."

"You did *what?*"

Anya's reaction turned Apa lighthearted again. He chuckled all the way past our field to the road.

Low mists followed us across the road and lingered in the strange new forest. I hesitated inside the barrier of woods. This was no longer my father's land.

The trees, the air, the very fallen leaves we trod upon seemed suddenly more mysterious. I took a deep breath of the moist air, then watched a single shaft of sunlight struggle through the thinning leaves above my head. Its haziness turned everything around us into a secret.

"It's going to be a perfect day, Apa," I whispered.

"What's that?" Apa was crouching by the moldering remains of a fallen tree. "Look, István. The stump mushrooms are ready."

I squatted next to him. "Can you eat them?"

"They're the only kind you can trust." He broke one off, rubbed it on his shirt, and separated a bit for each of us to taste. "Try it."

I did. It was strong, like the earth.

"We'll pick some for your mother on our return."

Then Apa was on his feet, striding off again deeper into the woods. I struggled through the brush behind him for a very long time until he stopped short. I scrambled around him. Our path was blocked by running water.

"What is this?" I asked. "I never knew it was here."

"It's the Tuckahoe River, although here where it just begins it is more like a wide stream." Apa pointed. "Look—the old cedar bridge the loggers built long ago is still in place."

I studied the worn logs laid at intervals across the river's bed, barely rising above the flow. Then I looked at the surrounding trees. "Is that a cedar?" I pointed at shiny green leaves, with berries forming beneath them.

Apa shook his head. "Cedars are conifers, like the pines. Their leaves are a spray of little pointy needles. That, István, is a holly tree, an evergreen."

"Evergreen? Does that mean—"

"It means exactly what it says. Holly leaves stay green all the year. Even better, the holly berries will be bright red by Christmas and we'll come and cut some for the house. No." He frowned a little sadly. "The cedars are all gone, long gone. Cut to make siding and roof shakes for many homes. This is scrub forest that takes its place—holly and laurel, and more pine."

"I see." Tree lessons were all very fine and good;

still . . . "When do we get to practice with the gun?"

Apa shifted the gun strap on his shoulder. "Across the river. There's something else to show you first."

I slipped across the mossy logs, passing two turtles basking in the pale sunlight now fighting the last of the mists. I followed my father along the far bank of the river, working my legs hard to keep up with his longer ones. Was it really necessary to go such a distance to find a safe place for the shooting? Would he never stop? I was so intent on my pursuit that when he did stop at last, I plowed right into his back. He smiled, picked me up, and plopped me down in front of him.

"There. What do you think of that?"

I stared at the shallow expanse of water before us. "What is it this time, Apa? The ocean?"

I scowled when Apa roared. We might have walked twenty miles to the sea, after all. It *felt* like twenty miles.

"No, István," he answered at last. "But you should figure it out for yourself."

I rubbed at a tired leg. "How?"

"Taste the water."

I considered the brownish water before me somewhat dubiously before crouching to cup a little in my hand. I sipped. "It's cold, and it tastes strange, Apa."

"That's the iron in it. But there's no salt, is there?"

I shook my head as I wiped my wet palm against my shirt front.

"There's your answer. It is not salty, there are no waves, and it does not go on forever. Therefore it is not the ocean. This is a *lake*," he declared with satisfaction. "One does not become seasick on a lake. And it has fish, too. This will be a good place for our practice."

There was not another soul around, so it was easy for Apa to set up a target along the shore of the lake. I watched as he rummaged in his pack and brought out two empty tin cans, already strung together with twine. He tied these to a low branch hanging out over the narrow shoreline. Then he measured paces from the target. Finally he scuffed a line in the sand with his boot heel.

"There. This will be a good place to start. We stand behind the line while shooting. As we become better, we will move the line farther back." He turned to me. "Is the gun pumped up?"

I nodded with enthusiasm. I'd pumped until there was not another pump left in my arms.

"Three shots each, István. Watch carefully while I take my turn first."

We practiced till we were out of BBs. I got used to the sudden jolt against my shoulder each time I pressed the trigger. The growing soreness was worth it for the occasional thrill of hearing the tiny *ping* of copper ball against tin when my aim was true. But as the supply of ammunition ran low, the gun became unexpectedly heavier and heavier. I didn't complain when Apa used the last BB and announced it was time for our lunch.

We sat on the sand and wolfed down Anya's food

in near silence. But it was a comfortable quiet. Through it you could hear things. There was the creak of branches in the wind. There was the occasional *plop* of a fish jumping from the lake to settle back down into spreading rings of water. Once, Apa nudged me and nodded to the shoreline not far from us. Together we watched a doe step daintily from the trees. Together we watched her take nervous sips from the lake before disappearing again as mysteriously as she'd arrived.

I grinned up at my father. "She didn't even notice us!"

"When you are very quiet, that is when you see things, István. Also, the wind is with us. It must be like that when hunting wild boar, too. The boar is a very wily animal for a pig. Very intelligent, and very dangerous."

"Did you really hunt wild boar?"

"Not exactly hunted . . ." He paused to consider his answer. "I was more like a guide, showing the way through the forests where I grew up."

"Was it truly beautiful there in the mountains,

Apa?" I asked. "Is that why Anya's father and brother stayed?" And got themselves killed in the Great War, I added to myself. Then, unable to help it, I blurted out, "And was that worth dying for?"

Apa shook his head. "No one knew the war was coming, son, but when it did, it became a matter of honor to fight. Your grandfather and uncle were patriots. They had no choice."

"But weren't you a patriot, too?"

"I had already made my own choices, István. They were not easy choices, for a man can never forget his motherland." He glanced over the lake, far beyond. Maybe as far as Hungary. "I do not regret my decisions. I made them for my children's future. For you, István."

"But I wasn't even born yet——"

"I knew you would be."

My father's certainty was amazing. It was also comforting. I wanted to ask more questions about wild boar and honor and the mountains of Hungary, but Apa was cocking his head and signaling for silence.

"Something else is coming. From where?"

I cocked my head, too, to listen better. Then I heard the new sounds: odd, echoing calls. "From the sky," I whispered.

"Yes."

When I saw what was coming over the lake, I was glad we were no longer shooting, glad we'd used up all our ammunition. It was a flock of lovely birds, flying quite low in a V formation. They flew so low I could see their long necks.

"The wild geese, István. Flying south for the winter from Canada."

"They're talking to each other!"

Apa nodded wordlessly and we watched them fly once, twice around our lake. As if deciding it was safe, the leader swooped lower yet, finally skimming over the cattails edging the far side, then elegantly across the surface of water, leaving a long wave behind him.

"It's like the wake of a ship, István," Apa murmured. "Cutting through the sea."

We sat for a long time, just looking. Then Apa

studied the sky. "We will find ourselves lost in the dark if we don't start back. It's time, son."

Anya never got her wild boar, but she did get a knapsack filled with mushrooms when we returned at dusk. She seemed quite satisfied with her hunters' catch.

NINE

A few nights later, the weasel tried for another one of our hens. This time, Apa got the weasel. I didn't know anything about it until the next morning, when I saw the skin hanging by the back door.

"Apa!" I'd been on my way out to school, but raced back into the warm kitchen, my breath still frosty. "Apa! When did that happen? Why didn't you call me, tell me?"

Apa set his coffee cup on the table. "For three nights I have been stalking the beast, István. Three *school* nights. Resting properly for your education must come first."

"But, but it would have been *educational* to help you catch him, Apa!"

"No." He shook his head definitively. "There was nothing new for you to learn from the experience."

"It would have been *fun!*" I protested.

"Killing is not fun. Only aristocrats in the Old World made a game of it, and they liked the game so much that they foolishly turned it into war. Here we will kill only from hunger or necessity. It was necessary to catch this weasel. It has now been accomplished."

He picked up his cup again, the subject closed. Until Sándor, still lingering over his breakfast, unwittingly opened it again.

"What's an *aristocrat*, Apa?"

Apa eyed my brother. "Shouldn't you be off to school with István?"

"There's enough time for you to tell me." Sándor scraped his nearly empty bowl stubbornly.

My father rubbed at the back of his neck. "In Europe it is one of the ruling class, one of those in charge. An important person. At least, it used to be."

"You were important, Apa," Irene innocently joined in. "Were you an aristocrat?"

"No. I was only educated. In Europe that wasn't enough. In America it is everything. Get your coats, both of you. You'll be late."

"What's education and aristocrats and war got to do with hunting weasels?" I spit out. "After our target practice together, Apa, I thought for sure we'd do that together, too!" I swerved toward my mother, seeking help. But there'd be no help from that quarter. Her head was bobbing in total agreement with Apa.

"It is done, István," Apa growled.

I slammed through the door again, the injustice of the situation making me hot all over. Anger was still with me until I ground to a halt beside the remains of my old foe, the weasel.

Somehow he was much smaller than I had remembered. My fingers reached out to touch the fur. His rich brown coat was still sleek, but those wicked yellow eyes had clouded over. I felt a sudden sorrow for the sharp intelligence, the wily depths that were now gone.

Head down, I trudged across the frost-hardened yard, trying to sort out the difference between education and learning, between understanding my father one minute and not at all the next. Between what made something alive, and what was lost when it was dead.

Apa took the weasel skin to Mr. Martin's store and traded it for something else. I learned this over the supper table that evening. My father finished his meal first, then turned to me.

"Is your homework done, István?"

"Almost," I muttered through a full mouth. I still hadn't quite decided to forgive my father for the weasel business.

"Finish it quickly. Then we will have a violin lesson—"

He caught my groan.

"You suddenly have something against music,

István? If you have something against music, perhaps what I brought home today from Mr. Martin's will not interest you."

I swallowed so quickly that I nearly choked. "I *love* music, Apa. What did you bring home?"

He folded his hands over the taut muscles of his stomach. "After your homework and after your music practice. If you work hard, then we shall see."

"Pista always works hard, Mihály," Anya broke in at last. "Don't torture the boy so."

"And what about me, Apa?" Sándor complained. "When will I get to see what you brought home?"

"When you are old enough to master violin scales."

Sándor shrugged and pushed back his chair. The last thing he wanted to do was learn how to play the violin, to play any kind of music. "I'm going to clean those motor parts I found at the dump."

"Sándor," Anya said, her voice rising. "You haven't been in that nasty dump again?" She was already talking to my brother's disappearing back. "Please don't get grease all over yourself before bedtime!"

she hollered after him. Then she snatched at little Mish, who'd slithered from his chair to trail after Sándor. "No motors for you tonight, young man. If you go upstairs with Irene, I'll come and tell you both a story when I'm finished here."

I downed my last spoonful of *gulyás* and reached for my schoolbooks.

What Apa had brought from the store was a booklet, a coil of wire, a small hunk of rock, a tiny brass cup, and a curious object that turned out to be earphones. I stared at the strange collection in silence. Was this why I had rushed through my homework? Was this why I had struggled so hard over my scales that my fingers were stiff and sore from stretching for unreachable strings? Was this what our wicked weasel had died for?

"What is it, Apa?" I finally asked.

"Nothing at the moment." He studied the odds and ends spread on the kitchen table, then glanced at my mother, who had returned from tucking in the little ones to fuss around the kitchen. She was probably curious, too. "Was there not an old cigar box somewhere around, Louisa? I think it will be vital to our experiment."

My mother rummaged behind things on a cupboard shelf and produced a box. I reached for it and opened the lid. The smell inside wafted over me, much nicer than the nasty smoke that actually came from cigars once they were lit. I was glad my father only smoked them for *occasions.*

"Are you finished inhaling the box, István?"

I slammed the lid shut and dropped the box on the table.

"Good. Now let us see what we have here." Apa fingered the collection of items, turning over the booklet. Finally I could read its title: *How to Make Your Own Crystal Set, in Easy Steps.*

"What is a crystal set?"

"A crystal set, István, is a *radio.*"

A radio! Some of my schoolmates were talking about radios! "Apa, you can hear things on them, from far away, and—"

"Just so, son," Apa placidly agreed. "If we are lucky, we'll pick up the station in Philadelphia."

By this time Anya had checked the baby and returned with her knitting. She sat down opposite us. "Fifty miles, Mihály? Is that possible?"

"All things are possible in this modern age, Louisa. I read in the papers that someone in Tokyo, Japan, had picked up a radio station broadcasting from Newark, New Jersey. Over nine thousand miles! I do not expect to travel such distances with our little crystal set, of course, but if we cannot receive from Philadelphia, then maybe we can hear Atlantic City. Someone said they were starting a radio station in Atlantic City."

"How far away is that, Apa?"

"Twenty-five miles, István. And the beauty of the crystal set is that it requires neither batteries nor electrical current. If we build it properly, we can snatch sound waves right out of the air." Then he was opening that booklet, which I suddenly found fascinating. *"Step one,"* he read aloud in English. *"Read all instructions first."* He looked up. "Sit next to me, son. Closer. You can help with some of the harder words."

·   ·   ·

Apa and I got to bed very late that night. Very late the next night, too. But the next night didn't matter, because it was Friday and there would be no school on Saturday. I was working very hard to keep my father interested in the radio project. Already I could tell the improvement in my violin playing. On Friday night Apa even let me read the notes on a sheet of music, and for the first time my scrapings began to sound like real music, although nothing near to what my father had played during our summer picnic. But I'd long since decided that what my father had played then for Anya was not music but magic—magic forever beyond me. Still, Apa seemed satisfied with tonight's performance.

He smiled while I tucked the violin back into its case. "Mozart," he said. "My son has played Mozart at last."

Maybe that was a start toward the magic. I squared my shoulders proudly. "And I'm only ten."

"Don't let it go to your head, István," Apa replied. "Mozart wrote that little piece when he was about five."

"Five? When he was *five*, like Irene?"

Apa patted my shoulder. "Never mind. You have remarkable skills building radios. I don't think young Wolfgang could have done such a thing."

That made me feel good all over again. I raced from the parlor. "Maybe we can finish it tonight, Apa."

"Maybe."

He followed me to the table and together we studied what we'd wrought thus far. Half of the cigar box was wound with tightly coiled black wire, and we'd mounted an arm-like slide on top of the wire. The little lump of rock had turned out to be the *crystal*, what Apa called the critical component. It was now fixed on the box next to the coil within the brass cup, with a thread-thin wire the booklet called a *cat's whisker* barely touching it at one end, while attached to the ear-phones at the other. I pulled open the instruction booklet.

"I think we only have to scrape enamel from the wire, Apa. So the slide can move over the copper beneath and control the frequency."

My father hunkered down next to me. "Why

don't you do the scraping, István. Your hands are steadier."

"There's nothing wrong with your hands, Apa—" I started. Then I grinned. He was letting me do the most important part. All by myself. I picked up a file and began.

"I don't understand, Apa!"

We'd been fiddling with the crystal set for hours. We'd rechecked every step in the instruction manual many times over. Still there was no sound from Philadelphia, no sound from Atlantic City. There was no sound at all.

Apa stroked his mustache thoughtfully. "Perhaps it is the night. Perhaps no one is broadcasting over the air."

"On Friday night? Friday night ought to be a *good* night for the radio."

"One would think . . ." Apa picked up the booklet again. He turned it over and stared at the back cover. "Wait. It talks here of an *antenna*. We never considered an antenna, István."

I grabbed for the booklet with a sinking heart. "It says: 'Since the crystal set depends entirely on the strength of the incoming signal to supply the power required for driving the headphones, it is essential that the signal applied to the receiver be as strong as possible. For this reason a long outdoor antenna is needed for satisfactory reception. This should be attached to a high elevation, with a ground pipe to complete the signal circuit.' What does that mean, Apa? And what is high around here? Nothing is high in South Jersey! Oh, for one of Anya's mountains!"

Apa yawned. "Probably we should sleep on the problem—"

"We can't go to sleep now! We're so close!"

Apa glanced at the clock and seemed startled. "Yes, so close to dawn that soon it will be unnecessary to wake up to light the lamps in the coop. Get to bed, son."

"But, Apa!"

He turned off the lamp, leaving us both in the dark. I grumbled all the way upstairs to my bed.

TEN

The frost was gone and the morning had warmed by the time Apa and I were ready to take on the antenna business. We stood outside the house considering elevations.

"The top of the roof, I think," Apa said, craning his neck. "Maybe attached to the chimney." He swiveled to study the feed house, our only other high elevation. "And perhaps another antenna above the second floor there, where we keep the grain. For good measure."

"That sounds wise, Apa. I'll fetch the ladder."

"Wait." He stopped me. "I'll help."

Soon my father was scrambling atop the very shingles of our roof, wire slung over one shoulder and tools poking from his rear pockets. He had a full audience for his labors. My brothers and sister were bunched together a few yards back from the kitchen door, necks stretched, solemnly watching. So were four cats. Unfortunately, I was bunched with all of them. Much to my dismay, Apa hadn't allowed me near the dangerous roof.

We breathed a sigh of relief as he made it to the chimney. We let out a little cheer as he hammered the first tack around a length of wire. That accomplished, Apa stopped. Carefully embracing the chimney with one arm, he turned to gaze off to the east. He seemed fascinated by what met his eyes.

"Apa! Apa!" Irene screamed. "What do you see?"

He glanced down most seriously. "It is really quite interesting. It proves what I thought two summers ago."

"What's that, Apa?" Sándor yelled up.

"You remember when I brought that ribbon home from the Great Egg Harbor Fair?"

How could we forget? The ribbon still hung on the wall of the kitchen. It had its very own place of honor, just below the steadily ticking Regulator clock. It proclaimed to the entire world—in *golden* letters—that Apa's chickens were *prize* chickens.

"Of course we remember, Apa," I called back. "Why?"

"After the judging, when I took that ride I told you about upon the Ferris wheel? From its very top I was almost certain I could see the chimney of *our* very own house." He paused with some drama, watching our open mouths. "Now I am sure. I can see the top of the Ferris wheel from here. It must be. The seats were all different colors. I sat in a red one, and—"

Sándor raced to the base of the ladder. "That I want to see." He darted up the rungs.

Apa hung tighter to the chimney and his face took on a very curious expression as Anya charged out the kitchen door. "Sándor! Get back down here at once!"

Sándor froze midway on his perch, like a bird.

Anya sent a look to Apa on the roof. "Really, Mihály. I heard everything you just said. You'll have the children breaking their legs and heads over your little joke!"

Sándor stared between Anya and the roof. "No Ferris wheel?"

"No Ferris wheel," Anya stated with finality. "Egg Harbor is seventeen miles away, son. How could anyone see that far? And the rides are taken away after the summer fair, anyway."

Sándor descended in a huff.

"But you can *hear* that far, Sándor," Apa called after him. "And even farther. Truly. Just wait until this antenna is finished."

After that, Apa's audience dwindled to one.

We only took off time enough to finish the most necessary chicken work that day. Yet Apa and I were still laying and burying wires in the falling darkness of early evening. Apa had been very quiet all day. No more jokes. I was sorry about that. But I worked in concentrated silence beside him. I handed him tacks, and tools, and made narrow grooves in the cold earth where he had traced the pattern for me. I patted the earth back down after the wire had been laid. Then I stamped upon it for good measure.

Anya was just calling us in to supper when the grounding—attaching our wire to a metal stake Apa had hammered into the earth—was complete. I clapped my hands in excitement.

"The antenna is finished. So is the grounding. We've poked the lead-in wire through a window to connect with the earphones. May we test the crystal set now, Apa?"

He stretched to his feet. "After we eat."

I jiggled impatiently. "I can't wait that long!"

"You must. Your mother would become upset again if we spoiled her hot meal."

"Oh."

I reached for my father's dirty hand as we walked back toward the house together. "I thought your joke was funny, Apa."

The distant look that had stayed on his face all through the afternoon changed into a smile that curled the ends of his mustache. "Did you see how well I had Sándor fooled?"

"Yes!" I giggled. "Irene believed it, too!"

"And you? What about you, István?"

"The view from the roof must be wonderful. I could see that red seat every bit as well as you, Apa."

Apa broke into laughter. We were still snickering with secret glee when we sat down to the table.

I ate so fast that all of the food lodged in a lump in my stomach. Then I had to sit there trying not to hug the sudden ache while everyone else took their good old time. If Anya thought I was sick, she'd pack me off to bed with Béla.

"Are you finished already, Pista?"

"Yes, Anya. It was delicious."

"István is right. It is delicious. I'll have another *palacsinta*, please, Louisa."

Anya smiled and passed the platter of meat-stuffed pancakes to my father. I moaned. We would be sitting here all night, as if nothing momentous were about to take place. The stations in Philadelphia and Atlantic City wouldn't wait for us forever. Their music would be gone, disappeared into the thin night air. There would be nothing for us to listen to with our fine new crystal set and antennas. I glared at Apa with ferocity as he carefully sliced into his pancake, begrudging him every bite and swallow. He took no notice. Or maybe he did. Halfway through the huge pancake, he looked at me.

"Perhaps we should practice on our violins first, István."

"No!" I screamed. It was a scream of panic edged with heartburn. I watched his eyebrows rise. "Tomorrow night, Apa. We'll practice twice the time tomorrow night."

"That is a promise?"

"Yes," I whispered, then finally hugged my stomach.

Anya had been watching everything. "I'm not sure all this excitement is healthy for the boy, Mihály. Not enough sleep for days, and—"

Apa finally swallowed his last bite. He pushed away his plate. "Still, he's worked hard. I think he deserves to try the radio tonight."

My cramp eased. "May I fetch the crystal set, Apa?"

"Yes, but I believe we shall test it in the parlor. Under the chandelier."

"Anything you say, Apa."

Anya only shook her head.

Yet Anya was settled on the stuffed couch in the parlor almost before we were ready. So were the other children, except for Béla. He was already in his crib, and not happy about it from the yelps of frustration descending the staircase. Maybe he wasn't too young to understand that something special was about to occur.

Apa glanced up the staircase, then turned to Anya. "Should we be successful, we will never hear the music after all. Not if those squalls continue."

With a sigh, Anya left her comfortable post to retrieve the baby. When all were settled again, Apa picked up the earphones and placed them over his head. He motioned for silence and nodded to me. It was my signal to try to find a station. I crouched over the wire-wrapped cigar box placed strategically in the middle of the rug. Directly under the chandelier, for luck. Brow furrowed, I concentrated on my task so hard that I was sure I'd be able to hear the sounds as well as Apa with his earphones. Suddenly Apa's hand was on my arm. My fingers froze.

"I've found something? You heard something?"

His grin was sufficient proof. Our radio worked! Everyone knew it at once. The hushed silence was replaced by a tremendous clamor of excitement as all the younger ones begged for the earphones. Apa shushed them.

"A little minute, please. István must listen next."

He placed the earphones on my head. Sure enough, there was *music* suddenly floating through my brain. It was a jaunty sort of music, not at all like scales, or Mozart, either. I listened for at least thirty seconds before I surrendered the contraption to Anya. Soon she was tapping her foot, then pulling baby Béla closer to her ear. He giggled and grabbed for the wires. Before disaster could happen, Anya relinquished the earphones to Sándor and Irene in turn. Irene danced to the music until Mish protested. When the phones were finally over his ears, he scowled.

"What's the matter?" Apa asked.

"No music!" Mish complained. "Only talking!"

"Let me hear." Apa snatched back the equipment. Then something strange happened. It was not another smile that crossed Apa's face. It was a look of wonder.

"What is it, Apa?" I yelled. "What's happening?"

He put a finger to his lips. "I cannot believe this."

"*What?*" we all roared.

He hushed us with a frown of concentration, then finally spoke. "It is the President of the United States himself. *Our* President. Mr. Calvin Coolidge." Apa seemed to focus within himself. "He is talking about the elections which will take place next Tuesday . . . about how important it is to vote."

The look of bliss remained on my father's face as he continued to listen. "Is not America a glorious place?" He hummed with satisfaction. "Where else is there such a thing as free elections for every man and woman to give their vote? Where else would the most important person in the world talk to his people as if they were neighbors and friends?"

Béla was asleep in Anya's lap, and Mish, too, curled up against her other side, before music was heard on our little radio again.

Thanks to our crystal set, the next week Apa could proudly announce to one and all that Mr. Calvin Coolidge would be President for another term. And this before the newspapers arrived on the train from Philadelphia announcing the same astounding fact. Apa firmly believed that his single vote at the election place set up at Martin's store was entirely responsible for this satisfactory state of affairs.

Of course, after listening to part of the President's speech through the earphones, Anya wanted to vote, too.

"But, dear heart," Apa reasoned with her, "you are not yet a proper citizen. Your English must be better before you can pass the naturalization test."

Anya's eyes flashed. "Then it shall become better. We'll speak more English at the table, and you will take me to Philadelphia for the test."

"Next summer," Apa promised. "In plenty of time for the elections next November."

"But those elections won't be for a president!" Anya cried out.

I'd never seen her so frustrated. "Why won't they be, Apa? Why won't Anya get to vote for Mr. Calvin Coolidge, too?"

"Aren't they teaching you civics at school, István? Only once every four years is there an election for a new president. Your mother will need to have a little patience."

"What about the rest of us?" I asked.

"You children will need to have more patience. Until you become twenty-one."

"Will we have to take the test?" Irene wanted to know.

Apa patted my sister's head. "No. You were lucky enough to be born citizens of the great United States of America. All of you."

With that, the subject was dropped. But Anya studied her Hungarian–English Dictionary harder than ever. She faithfully underlined new words memorized each day. Anya had the book propped open above the stove, and would seriously turn from definitions to bubbling pots of food and back again. She also studied her little book about the history of the United States. And she listened to the crystal set every night. She became impatient with the almost constant dance music. She wanted to hear people talking, so she could learn the proper way to say things.

The rest of us thought the music was just fine. For a while it took the place of violin lessons each night. But not for long enough.

ELEVEN

There was a new game at school. Usually during morning recess everyone ran outside to kick a ball around the worn diamond-shaped infield where we played baseball in the spring. Kickball used the same rules as baseball and was easier to play on the hard, half-frozen earth. But the newly invented game was rougher than plain old kickball, and the older boys played it with relish. They called it "Jersey Devil Ball." As soon as the ball was kicked, the boy chosen to be "devil" came racing out of nowhere and tried to tackle the runner to the ground between bases.

"What is this *Jersey Devil?*" I complained, limping

off the field after my first experience at being viciously attacked. "Where did it come from?"

Big Nick Besz made horns over his head and leered down at me. "He was born in the woods just down the road, and he comes out of them every few years when he gets good and hungry." He bent nearer. "Sometimes for eggs. But sometimes for small children's blood. *Nyyaaaah!*"

I jumped.

One of Nick's pals joined him. "The devil's got two pointy horns sticking out of his horsy head, a long tail, hooves, and bat wings." He waved his arms. "All on a man's body. My pa says he had a normal mother when he was born way back, before the Revolution. But he was her thirteenth baby and she was fed up on kids. So when he started getting born, she cursed him, and he come out funny like that."

I looked at Nick for confirmation of these details.

"It's all true, Steve, except Pete forgot the most important part."

"What?" I asked.

Nick was almost on top of me now, and whispered in my ear. "When the Jersey Devil decides to leave the woods the way he just has, trouble always comes with him. *Big trouble.*"

I wasn't the only one with tales of the Jersey Devil nudging at the back of his head. Our supper table was filled with them that night.

Sándor spit it out first. "Is it true about the Jersey Devil coming back, Apa?"

Apa raised his eyebrows. "A devil? Where have you heard such things, Sándor?"

"Where else but school?"

"Certainly not from your teacher!"

A look of scorn crossed my brother's face. "Course not. Only my classmates. They say old Mrs. Oze saw it come from the woods behind her house just two nights ago. It smelled terrible and made her dog drop dead on the spot!"

Apa reached for his glass. "I suspect it was a skunk responsible for Mrs. Oze's dog. It was a very ancient dog, almost as ancient as Mrs. Oze herself."

"Well, then," Sándor countered, "what about those footprints people saw by the cemetery behind the church? They were hoofprints, but way bigger, like a bear——"

"An occasional bear has been known to wander in this direction, Sándor."

I glanced at Anya to see how she was taking these revelations. My mother was busy watching Mish's eyes grow larger and larger. "I thought we'd left such superstitious nonsense back home in Transylvania. Please change the subject, Mihály."

Apa opened his mouth but didn't get to do any subject changing. Irene joined the conversation first.

"Sándor didn't tell all of it," she solemnly declared. "That devil eats raw eggs. I don't want to go in the chicken coop anymore."

"Don't be dumb," Sándor shot back. "He likes his eggs fried, by the dozen. And there's some old judge in Egg Harbor he likes to eat them with."

"A judge?" I asked. This was a new piece of information. "If the Jersey Devil is friends with a judge, then he should know the difference between right and wrong, and shouldn't go around sucking blood from children——"

"Enough!" Apa ordered. "You begin to make this devil sound like Dracula himself!"

"Dracula?" Sándor's head jerked up. "Who's Dracula?"

Anya had already left the table, and was busily trying to hustle Irene, Mish, and Béla out of the kitchen. Over Irene and Mish's protests, she turned to Apa. "Be careful of things you say, Mihály. As you can see, little heads are impressionable."

Sándor and I only hitched our chairs closer to Apa's. Despite the chill down my spine, this was becoming more interesting every moment. "You can't stop now, Apa," I said. "You really have to answer Sándor's question."

Apa was carefully wiping his mustache with his napkin. Too carefully. He was trying to think of a way out. He was also waiting for the youngest ones to get safely beyond earshot. But he was well and truly cornered this time. He gave in.

"What is there to say? I was only referring to legends that used to float around Transylvanian Hungary about Count Dracula, also known as Vlad the Impaler—"

"What's an *Impaler*?"

"Never mind, Sándor. Let us just say that this Vlad Dracula helped defend Europe against the terrible Turkish invasion in the fifteenth century. He was Romanian, not Hungarian. We Hungarians fought the Turks valiantly ourselves, but not in unexpected midnight raids as Count Dracula did. Because he went about his business with such bloodthirsty enthusiasm, beating even the Turks at their own game, strange tales have grown around his memory. Some even say that he is still alive, but only at night—"

"Like a bat!" I exclaimed. "This Jersey Devil comes out at night the same way, and he even has bat wings. Do you think he's related to Dracula?"

Apa extricated himself from between Sándor and me. "I know nothing about this New Jersey creature. However . . ." He gave us a stern look. "However, if you promise never to bring the name up again in front of the younger children, I will consult with Mr. Martin on the subject."

"Tomorrow?" I cried.

"Yes, tomorrow. Before things get out of hand."

"I promise." I turned to Sándor. "You promise, too."

"Did you see the look on silly Irene's face?" Sándor grinned. "And how scared Mish got?"

I jabbed him in the ribs. "Promise Apa. Now!"

Sándor rubbed his side. "All right, then, I promise."

"Good. Then Apa can take care of it."

Apa and my brother left the kitchen, but I lingered by the warmth of the stove, shivering a little despite its heat. I had been careful—very, very careful—not to mention the last thing Big Nick had said to me this morning. What did I care about smells and footprints, or even a little lost blood? Remembering the Heller boys last summer, the threat of *big trouble* was what bothered me.

It was unusual for Sándor to wait for me after school. But the next afternoon, there he was, sitting on the steps in front of the white wooden building. I glanced around for my sister.

"Where's Irene?"

"I sent her on home ahead of us so we could talk about this devil business."

"By herself? Now? Didn't you hear about what happened to the Burkitts' dog last night?"

He gave his typical shrug. "So somebody is fed up with the meaner dogs around here. Now they've got a good excuse to get rid of them."

"You didn't hear how it was torn apart?"

He began to look a little worried, then jumped off the steps and began to run. I followed the worn path over the train tracks and raced after him all the way home. We rounded the house, both sliding to a halt by the kitchen door.

Irene was sitting on the back stoop with a cookie in her hand. It was a crescent-shaped *kifli*, the kind Anya said had been invented after the Turks were chased from Hungary for good and final.

"I got to test the first *kifli*, hot out of the oven, because I got home first. So there." Irene carefully bit it in two.

My brother and I stood there waiting for our

heartbeats to slow down, saying nothing, either to our sister or to each other. When mine began to feel almost normal again, I dropped my books and swiped the sweat from my face. Instead of begging for *kiflis*, I went in search of Apa. Sándor followed me like a shadow. Our father was in the feed house, beginning to mix the next week's worth of mash.

"So." He tore open a hundred-pound bag of cornmeal and spread it in the center of the floor. "You're home."

We shuffled from one foot to the other.

"If you've come to help, drag over a bag of bran, please, while I deal with the oatmeal."

My brother and I lugged the heavy bag from its pile. Soon Apa added it to the mound. Then he added the wheat and the wheat middlings and the alfalfa meal. Now the pile was more like my idea of a mountain. Apa threw a little salt, grit, and charcoal on the very peak. At last he reached for his shovel and began to mix it all together. When that was accomplished, Sándor and I helped to scoop it all into the large storage bin. We did all this with only grunts and a few comments—mostly under Sándor's breath. Finally the mountain was gone and Apa leaned on his shovel and inspected us.

"So," he repeated. "You heard about the Burkitts' dog. As has the entire world." He stopped, and we waited some more. "Luckily," Apa finally continued, "I consulted with Mr. Martin today—"

"What did he say?" I couldn't hold the question back any longer.

Apa frowned at the interruption. I bit my tongue and slowly counted in my head to ten. Then eleven. At *twelve*, Apa began once more.

"As I was trying to explain. It seems the Burkitts' dog liked very much to tease the bull kept by the Yanche family. When the dog went to renew his program yesterday afternoon, the bull reached his limit. He gored the dog."

"The bull did it?" I asked.

"In the afternoon?" Sándor continued.

"Yes. The bull did it in the afternoon. Your *Jersey Devil* did *not* do it at night."

"It's not *my* Jersey Devil, Apa!"

"Mine, either," Sándor protested.

"Nevertheless," Apa said, "Mr. Martin agreed there were tales. He also agreed these tales begin to circulate whenever something unexpected chooses to happen around here. Your creature has even been blamed for wars! Not only the American Revolution but also something called the War of 1812, which I confess I never heard about before. And then there was the more recent Great War. The Jersey Devil was blamed for that one, too." Apa paused. "You understand what this means, boys?"

Sándor and I both shook our heads.

"Then I will explain for you. This *Jersey Devil* is nothing but a *scapegoat*, something used to take the blame for bad things. He is make-believe, fictitious, a mere figment of the imagination. Something that preys on simple minds to cause hysteria."

My head reeled at all the new expressions Apa was using. I'd never heard them, but the overall idea got through. "So he hasn't really come out of the woods?"

"No." Apa pounded the hard dirt floor with his

shovel for emphasis. "Absolutely not. He never came out of the woods, because he never existed. He never was born to Mrs. Leeds in the swamps down the road near Estellville. The only place he exists is in the minds of simple, uneducated people. People who have nothing better with which to fill their brains." Apa gave us both a final, fierce look, a look that turned his eyebrows into one long line across his brow. "And this closes the discussion on the Jersey Devil in my household. Forever. Is that understood?"

Sándor blinked. "Yes, Apa."

I nodded. Then I left the feed house to stare out toward the woods. The forest stood there in a wintry, brooding mass, not at all welcoming as it had been for our summer picnic. A lone crow cawed. I plunged my hands into my pockets. It was only woods. Still and all, strange things had happened. Could Apa banish the Jersey Devil just by saying so? Did Apa really have that kind of power?

TWELVE

Whether the Jersey Devil was a mere figment, tale, or whatever, Sándor and I saw to it that Irene was escorted home from school thereafter. Religiously. Then the talk at school turned to new subjects of interest, such as an early snowfall that eliminated any ballgames whatsoever for a while—and also put everyone in mind of the more distant coming of Christmas. Even Apa himself became involved with these considerations.

It began on a day when he came home from talking business at the store. He marched directly to the parlor where our instruments were kept and began to apply rosin to the bow of his violin. He rubbed it on with such intensity that I immediately knew our radio vacation from painful music, from real music, was over. Apa pointed to the shorter bow for my three-quarter violin, and I followed suit. I waited for his announcement. I knew it would come soon. It did.

"There is to be a concert at church to welcome Advent, István. I have been asked to participate."

I tucked bow under arm and reached for my instrument in silence, waiting for the rest of his news.

"It is an honor. And you will be joining me in this honor."

I twanged a string in dismay. It was flat. "But, but—"

"Nothing difficult for you, son. We'll polish up that little Mozart piece you have been working on."

"But, Apa!" He meant that impossible sonata with the quick fingering. "In front of all those people?"

"It will be a good experience. A positive experience. Music is not meant to be a solitary pleasure. It should be shared."

I thrust my violin under my chin, close to tears. It was hard enough to recite at school in front of Mr. Strick and my classmates. However could I survive such an experience as playing badly in front of the entire congregation of our church? My first note came out particularly sour. Maybe this was the big trouble that old Jersey Devil had been brewing. He wanted everyone at church to suffer. Hadn't his footprints been seen in the very cemetery behind it?

But my father didn't give me time for either tears or superstitions. Thereafter we practiced twice as hard and twice as long each night, with Apa adding little lectures.

"The secret of a good left-hand technique is in how one holds down the fingers, István."

"Yes, Apa."

He frowned. "Saying yes does not make your technique improve. Watch so: one uses a little pressure for the first finger; a little more for the second finger; a little more each for the third and fourth."

I tried. Apa's fingers came down on mine.

"Always only a slight pressure for the first finger. Remember."

As the time before the concert rapidly disappeared, we practiced three times as long. My mother avoided the parlor. My brothers and sister crept around us quiet as mice on their way upstairs to bed. From the quick looks they gave me, I saw only relief in their eyes. Relief that it was *me*, and not *them*, being tortured.

And then the Sunday dawned.

It was a cold day. There was the look of fresh snow in the sky. I poked my head from the bedroom window, studying the signs. "Let it snow," I prayed. "Let it snow so hard and fast that it becomes a blizzard." Then everyone would have to stay at home. The concert would be canceled. I would be saved.

All morning the same prayer went through my head. At lunch I couldn't eat my mother's chicken soup. Not even with my favorite fat noodles bobbing around the top of my bowl. The snow hadn't come.

My silent prayer changed. Now it became a complaint. Why did the only church in town have to hold services at two o'clock in the afternoon? If it were in the morning, the concert would already be finished and done with. Why did our church have to be a mission church? Why did the priest have to come to us only after he'd finished with the other towns along the way?

Then another thought struck me. Maybe that big old car Father Pierot drove would have a flat tire. It takes a long time to change a flat tire. He'd be too late for church. The concert would have to be canceled. I splashed my spoon into my bowl with glee. A noodle flipped out and flew across the table, landing in Irene's lap.

"*Ow!*"

She shimmied until we heard a splat on the floor. Anya's fat noodles were substantial.

"What're you doing, Pista? This is my Sunday dress. And now you've gone and ruined it!"

"Have not!"

"Have too!"

"Children!" Anya was already bending over my sister, rubbing at the spot on her dress. "I think it will be all right, Irene. It landed mostly on your apron." She straightened to look at me. "Really, Pista. You're behaving like the baby today!"

What could I say? I hung my head.

Then we were walking along the road to church. All of us in a row with Apa leading and my mother just behind, with Béla in her arms. Up the long road surrounded by the winter-bare branches of oak trees. Across the railroad tracks. Past the schoolhouse toward Holy Nativity Church, sitting just beyond. A few snowflakes fell out of the steel-gray sky. I glared at them. Too little, too late. I gathered my violin case to my chest. It gave me no comfort. I was going to have to go through with the concert after all. Of a sudden thought, I trailed behind the family, then ducked around the church building for a quick peek at the cemetery. Maybe there'd be a sign there. Maybe some telltale hoof-prints . . .

"István!"

Apa had me by the collar. "The entrance is this way."

I made it inside much against my will, then forgot my troubles for the moment. The little white church looked like Christmas already. The windows and altar were hung with greens. Candles softly glowed atop snow-white linens. Someone had laid out the Nativity set earlier than usual in the farthest corner of the sanctuary. Not only did the whole place look wonderful, but all the people who rarely went to church except for the really important times had come. Nearly every seat was taken. That made me remember again.

I watched Anya squeeze into the last pew, piling as many children as possible onto her lap. I watched Apa stride proudly toward the altar. Me, I waited by the door, rooted to the spot. Coming from behind, a few more men with instruments walked around me and up the aisle. Apa turned and beckoned. Nothing—not even the Jersey Devil—could save me now. I licked my chapped lips, cleared my parched throat, and followed.

The priest poked his head from the room behind the altar. In a moment he appeared in full vestments. Church began.

It was after the Gospel that we were meant to play, instead of the usual long sermon. I stood with the musicians to one side of the altar all the way through the reading, tensely clutching my violin by its neck. When I got up the nerve, I raised my eyes to look at the audience—all the way back to Anya and the rest of our family.

That's when I saw Mish squirm from my mother's skirts. She was so busy hanging on to Béla and Irene that she didn't notice him scoot off. Neither did Sándor, whose expression told me he was a thousand miles away, probably racing automobiles with Barney Oldfield. I noticed, though. Where was Mish going? To sneak up the side aisle to admire the Christmas stable with its wonderful sheep and camels? No, he was slipping into the vestibule behind. I forgot about my concert for another moment as I watched him disappear with some satisfaction.

Mish was smart. He was bored and wasn't putting up with it anymore. If only I had just turned four, like he had. I could be following him—

A shrill squeal cut through the last words of the Gospel. It was followed by a bone-breaking clatter and a resounding crash. The congregation, still numbed by the reading, did nothing. I quickly set my violin on the floor and raced down the aisle. People stared at me like I was crazy—even Anya, who registered my flight, then immediately began to count children. When Mish began to howl, they all caught on.

But I got to him first. Someone had left the cellar trapdoor open, the one that went down to the furnace. And Mish had fallen right into it. I slid down the opening into the darkness. There was a little halo of orange light coming from the door of the furnace. It was enough to see my brother writhing on the hard-packed dirt floor. His screams had changed to a steady moaning.

"Mish! Are you all right?"

"Pista!" At the sight of me, he sniffed back tears, then let out a final howl, just for good measure.

I sighed with relief. If he could still make that much noise, I figured he would live. I hefted him from the floor and raised him to the arms waiting above. Then I found the rungs of the ladder and climbed out. The trapdoor was closed behind me. Very firmly.

Apa was present by this time. The priest was, too, and a whole crowd behind them. Mish's arms and legs were thoroughly examined, with much bending of knees and elbows. From the fascinated expression on his face, I could tell my brother was no longer bored.

"Well," Father Pierot announced at last, "the lad seems to be in fighting form after his mishap. Why don't we all settle ourselves again, and offer a prayer of thanks for his deliverance. Then we can proceed with our musical interlude and move on to the Communion."

I swallowed hard at the priest's words. Obviously, nothing was about to stop this concert. And as the youngest musician, I was scheduled to perform first. I finally accepted the inevitability of it all. If this was the worst the Jersey Devil could do, maybe I could handle it. I marched back up the aisle beside Apa. My violin was waiting where I'd set it down. I retrieved it, dusted the curves of wood with my sleeve, and, after Mish's deliverance prayer was over, turned to my father. He gave me one firm nod. I bowed toward the audience, the way Apa had taught me. I tucked under my chin the tiny scrap of silk Apa had presented me with before we'd left home. The violin followed. I raised my bow and began.

The sounds that came from my instrument didn't seem to belong to me. I heard them through eyes squeezed tightly shut; heard the notes rising through the church, up to the steeple. They seemed to float on forever, amazingly strong and true. Then Apa's hand was on my shoulder and I lowered my bow and opened my eyes. Apa was smiling with pride. The audience was clapping. I guess Mozart survived.

I bowed this time with assurance, then sent my own special smile down the aisle to my little brother. Mish had scared all the fear out of me. Afterward, Apa said nothing, but he smoked a cigar all the way home.

THIRTEEN

Two days after the famous concert, Apa arrived at the breakfast table with a queer expression on his face. He gingerly lowered himself into his chair as Anya turned from her stove.

"No kiss this morning, Mihály?" She paused, her smile fading. "What is it, husband?"

"Nothing, dear heart. Just this odd . . ." He winced and grabbed for his side below his stomach.

I stopped eating. All of us children did. Anya stood like a rock, still holding in her hands the heavy iron frying pan with Apa's eggs. They were perfect little suns, just the way Apa liked them. But the sun had gone from my mother's face.

"There is a pain down there? Lower than the heart. Your appendix?"

"Perhaps." He groaned.

I felt my eyebrows rise. Sándor's did the same. Irene grabbed for her ever-present doll and hugged it to her body. None of us had ever heard Apa groan before.

"No eggs, I think," Apa managed to continue. "No breakfast at all. Perhaps I should see a doctor."

"Pista." Anya came alive to give the order fast. "Don't worry about school just now." She slammed the pan back onto the stove. "Run to Mr. Martin and see if he will drive your father to a doctor."

I gulped, shoved away my own half-finished eggs, and raced for a coat and the road.

"Appendix," I whispered to myself over and over. "Appendix." My legs took me past the winter woods in record time. I didn't need to think to urge their speed. What was this strange appendix that could make my father groan? That could make me more frightened than a violin concert before a million people?

I gasped as I reached the railroad tracks. There it was necessary to stop for a moment. It was necessary to bend over to try to ease the stitches needling through my own side. But these pains were not caused by my *appendix*. I was sure of it. I kicked out my legs again and followed the tracks to the station, then across the empty road to the store. I banged through the door, burning hot and huffing for breath. Would Mr. Martin be here? I could hardly see for the sweat dripping past my eyes. I rubbed a coat sleeve across my face. The pickle barrel sat in the same spot as always. And the potbelly stove, roaring with life.

"Mr. Martin! Sir!"

There he was, thank goodness, in his usual place by the counter. He looked up from his account books. "Stephen? What's the matter?"

"It's Apa—my father. It's his *appendix*!" I staggered on legs that felt like noodles, puffing, hugging my chest, hoping I wouldn't break into tears. Mr. Martin didn't give me time to disgrace myself. He got up at once.

"Is it bad?"

I nodded.

"Mother!" he yelled behind the counter and waited for the old lady to poke her head from the back room. When she saw me, she scurried out, eager for any gossip.

"Mike's gone sick," Mr. Martin explained. "Maybe his appendix. I'd better fetch him in the auto. Hold the train if it's early. We might have to send him to the hospital in Philadelphia."

Then I was riding in Mr. Martin's new Chevrolet. Right up in the front seat next to him. Everything was shiny, and it even smelled new. But I couldn't enjoy it. Not a bit.

By the time we got to our house, Apa was doubled over on the couch in the parlor. My brothers and sister were huddled on the stairs, silently watching from across the room. Even Béla sat dangling his short legs, a thumb stuck in his mouth.

Anya was standing under the chandelier, wringing the hem of her apron.

Mr. Martin took one quick look at Apa, gave a little poke that made my father yelp, and proclaimed, "Yup, it's his appendix all right." He turned to Anya.

"I'm going to drive your husband directly back to catch the train. I'll wire the hospital at the other end to expect him."

Anya nodded as if she'd caught all that, but looked bewildered just the same. After we'd settled Apa in the backseat of the Chevrolet and Mr. Martin roared off, I explained it all again.

"I thought so," Anya breathed as we climbed the porch steps and entered the front door. "Thank you, Pista." Then she slowly studied all of us children. "You're late for school! Get on your coats, quickly!"

"But, Anya—" I began to protest.

"But nothing." She was already buttoning up Irene. "We will make believe your father has gone again to Philadelphia for work. Like last spring. We'll just carry on." I caught her voice breaking. "We'll manage," she finished.

． ． ．

It was a hard week before Apa came home again on the train. It seemed I barely fell asleep before it was time to wake for the four o'clock lighting of the chicken coop. Then I hardly dozed off before it was necessary to rise again. This time I would drag Sándor from bed, too, and together we cleaned the hens' water pans and fed them their mash before breakfast. Apa usually did the feeding and watering later, but Apa was in Philadelphia.

Sándor and I hurried home after school to repeat the same chores, while Irene and Mish collected eggs. Next the eggs had to be polished and weighed and packed in our feed house—also work Apa used to do. I suspect we did not do it as well. Irene tried really hard, but she kept dropping eggs. There they would lie, little yellow puddles on the hard dirt floor, while my sister tearfully mourned over every loss. The cats had already caught on to who was now in charge. They hung around, ready to pounce on each new disaster. At least it saved me from having to clean up the mess. But eventually most of the eggs got packed. Then it would be suppertime. After supper I tried to do my homework while Anya settled the younger ones in bed.

As each day passed into the next, and the weekend disappeared to turn into another school night, my head began nodding lower and lower over my books. One night, my head banged into the table. With a start, I pulled it up to find Anya sitting across from me, watching.

"Almost done," I mumbled, rubbing at my eyes. "All that's left is to practice my violin scales."

"Don't worry about your violin, Pista," Anya said.

"But I have to, Anya. What would Apa think?"

"Your father . . ."

I watched my mother rub at her own eyes. They looked awfully red through the lamplight.

"Your father," she continued, "cannot expect the impossible."

"But we managed everything in the spring, Anya, when Apa went to Philadelphia for work."

"That was in the spring. It was before we had almost a thousand laying hens. This is winter. You're only a child, son. Go to sleep."

I glanced down at my notebook. Strange, I thought I'd accomplished more work than what stared back at me. The arithmetic problems were only half completed. I flipped to an earlier page. And my penmanship exercises were splotched and unsteady.

"I haven't finished," I whispered. "Mr. Strick will use his ruler on me tomorrow."

"Mr. Strick will do no such thing. Go to sleep!"

Stranger and stranger. When I dragged myself into my classroom the next day, I sat down and prepared to present my unfinished homework. I set out the lined pages. I carefully noted each imperfection to myself. Then I spread out my hands, palms up in readiness for my punishment. Mr. Strick preferred no surprises.

The teacher stopped by my desk and studied my notebook. I saw the ever-present ruler twitch in his grasp. Time stopped for a long moment as my up-turned palms began to itch. Then he just nodded and moved farther down the aisle. I stared at my waiting hands. In disbelief, I finally stilled their trembling and picked up my pen.

We didn't know Apa was coming. We didn't even know what all had happened to him in Philadelphia. He just arrived on the evening train exactly one week after he'd gone. One full week during which all any of us could remember was his last painful groans at the breakfast table. Anya had given up completely on trying to make believe it was spring and Apa was looking for work. It was the memory of those groans that had kept the farm running.

Mr. Martin delivered him to us as we were sitting down to supper.

"Apa!"

"Mihály!"

All six of us sprang at him as he came through the kitchen door. Then we backed off. Apa was wobbling on his feet, leaning hard into Mr. Martin. And his face was a very peculiar color, even in the soft kerosene light of the kitchen. Sort of yellowish . . .

"Here's your man," Mr. Martin announced with

forced cheerfulness. "A little weary after the hospital and the long train ride back, but good as new soon. Maybe if you set him up on the couch . . ."

Anya had taken everything in and was already on her way for fresh linens. Sometime in the course of making Apa comfortable in the parlor, Mr. Martin disappeared, not even waiting for our thanks. Then there was Apa lying there, smiling up at us.

"I am just a little sore and tired," he murmured. "But it is so good to be home."

FOURTEEN

It was going to take a while, that was all. I was sure
of it.

Apa's operation had made him very weak.
He probably should have stayed longer in the hospital, but he wanted to be home before Christmas.

"We have evergreens to collect from the woods,
István," he confided to me the next morning. "Remember that holly? Its berries should be red by
now. And we'll need a nice little pine tree for the
parlor . . ."

I stared at my father propped up on pillows. His

face was even more yellow in the daylight, and the very whites around his eyes had turned yellow, too. He didn't look anywhere near being able to hike off into the woods anytime soon. But I smiled. Apa at home in any condition was better than Apa off in Philadelphia. And the holly berries should be red again next Christmas if he couldn't quite manage the trip for this one. "That will be wonderful, Apa. Maybe we should take Sándor with us this time, to help carry things."

"An excellent suggestion." He eased farther back into the pillows and his eyes closed. "I'll just nap a little, while you go to school."

"That's a good idea, Apa."

Sándor and Irene had already set off for school, and I went for my coat, but I knew I wouldn't be returning to classes very soon. Even if Mr. Strick excused me from my homework, which was what he seemed to be doing, I still needed more free time at home. My mother couldn't possibly deal with Mish and Béla and the chickens—and Apa. She just didn't have enough hands and arms. Anya watched me set off for the hens without a word about my education.

With all the good chicken soup Anya spooned into him, my father should have gotten better fast, but he didn't. The little ones tiptoed around him, not quite sure of what was happening. Anya tried to keep the baby in the kitchen, but Béla was working on his legs. I remembered Mish going through the same thing. One second Béla would be crawling, the next tottering up on his feet. And the next he'd be going so fast you'd have to tackle him to keep him from doing mischief. Now he'd disappear like lightning into the parlor, then stop short at seeing Apa on the couch, as if he were surprised by the sight each and every time. His giggles would vanish and I'd have to fetch him back to the kitchen fast, so he wouldn't yowl Apa awake.

Before he came home from the hospital, I thought nothing could be worse than hearing Apa groan. I was wrong. Watching him lie there quietly in the parlor was worse.

I escaped for a little while that afternoon. I just dumped the empty mash bucket and headed off across the field for the woods. Along the way I stopped long enough to collect pocketfuls of pebbles. They were hardly big enough to be called stones, yet at the edge of the woods I imagined them to be boulders. Huge boulders fallen from a great mountain. I threw these boulders into the woods, one after the other, harder and harder. What was I trying to hit? The Jersey Devil who had finally succeeded with his big trouble? I yelled with each pebble from my pockets. Louder and louder. It wasn't in Hungarian and it wasn't in English. It wasn't in any language that I knew. It was loud, though, and when there was nothing left to throw and nothing left to howl, I knew that devil had already done his worst and was long gone. I went back across the field to finish feeding the hens.

After a few days a doctor came from Vineland, fifteen miles away, to inspect my father. Anya and I hovered out of the way in the kitchen until the examination was completed. When the doctor came out at last, Anya asked haltingly in English, "How is . . . my husband?"

The doctor shook his head. "I'm afraid he has an infection. Those bandages will need to be changed several times a day. Also, he's contracted jaundice. Perhaps they should have removed his gallbladder in Philadelphia while they were at it."

There was something else to remove besides an *appendix*? I shuddered to think of my father, slowly becoming hollow on the inside of his strong body— what *had* to become a strong body again very soon.

"Is there . . . medicine?" Anya tried.

"I'll leave some pills, but there's no guarantee . . ."

No guarantee? What did that mean? We didn't get our money back if the pills didn't work? I watched Anya pay the doctor from the dwindling supply of dollars in the coffee canister. Where had all the money gone? The can had been so full before Apa got sick! I remembered Apa counting it out one night just before the concert, laying it in neat piles.

"This one," he said, "is for an electric generator. No more waking up at four in the morning for the hens, son. There will be a little timer box which automatically turns on the lights whenever we wish. There will be light everywhere. Even in our chandelier!"

Before I could express my enthusiasm, he continued.

"This pile"—he started another one—"is the beginning of our very own automobile."

My eyes widened. A real automobile! That was better than electricity. I'd wake up before dawn forever to own an automobile. "A Model T, Apa?"

He gave me a look of scorn. "When I purchase an automobile, István, it will be the best!"

"A Packard?" I breathed.

Apa rocked back in his chair grandly. "Maybe even an *Auburn*."

I whistled. "What else, Apa?"

"And this pile . . ." He stopped to grin at me, then stacked the remaining notes, and all the loose coins, too. "This pile is for Christmas coming. And maybe another special event that is also coming very soon, just before Christmas. I think you know which event I mean."

Christmas presents! And the birthday I'd been anticipating but had been afraid to even think about. Only a few days before Christmas that would happen. I couldn't help it. I blurted out, "Maybe I could have a penknife, the same as yours, Apa? So you could teach me some of your tricks, like how to peel an orange properly, or how to make a puzzle from an apple. The way your father taught you?"

Apa's face had taken on a secretive look. "Who knows the mystery of Christmas, István? Or of other, very special events. One must live in hope and wait."

Now I lived in hope and waited as I watched the doctor leave. But it was no longer the penknife I prayed for. It was to have my father back again, the way he used to be.

To make Apa feel better, I made believe I was still going to school every morning. Decked out in coat and scarf, I lined up by the couch with the others for Apa's inspection.

"The mathematics, István. How does it go?"

"We're doing decimals and percentages, Apa."

He coughed. It looked as if it hurt. "And you understand them?"

"I did a problem on the blackboard, Apa. In front of the whole class." I grinned at the memory, even though it had happened while my father was away. "I got it right, then explained why it was right."

Apa's mustache curled with his small smile of triumph. "Mathematics is the basis of everything. You will do great things one day." He turned his head toward Sándor. "What about you, son?"

Sándor had been trying to edge from the room. He froze. "I fixed Mr. Strick's car engine yesterday. He just had a dirty spark plug."

Apa's fingers lying on the quilt twitched. "So. When we have our Auburn, you will be in charge of the motor."

"Truly, Apa?" Sándor beamed.

"Truly." Apa's eyes settled on Irene. "And you, daughter. What have you to report from school?"

Irene had been busily wrapping her scarf around her doll. She stopped fiddling to think hard. "Miss Cain told us stories yesterday, Apa. About the Indians who used to live here, before we came. They were very brave. She showed us pointy things they hunted with. *Arrowheads.*"

"And what were they called, these Indians?"

Irene thought even harder. She squeezed her doll and her face puckered up. I knew she couldn't answer.

"You remember, Irene," I helped out. "It's a good name. The Lenni—"

"Lenape!" she crowed.

"Yes," Apa agreed. "I, too, have found their arrowheads . . ." He paused, and I noticed the beads of sweat forming on his forehead. "Along the railroad tracks . . ." he tried.

"We'll learn even more today, Apa." I pushed Sándor and Irene toward the door.

"Good," Apa sighed.

I waited on the road in front of the house till I was sure my brother and sister were on their way to school. Then I rounded the house as silently as a stalking Lenni-Lenape to take on the chickens. My face was stiff and my eyes burned, but Indians didn't cry.

In the evening, I settled the earphones of the crystal set around Apa's head. I sat next to him while he listened, straining to catch something of the broadcast. But after a short while he seemed to tire of it and motioned for me to take it away.

"The program wasn't good tonight, Apa?"

"There was static," he murmured. "Maybe a storm is coming."

I set the radio carefully atop the mantel, next to the wedding portrait. What to do next? Out of desperation, I picked up my violin.

"Shall I play my scales, Apa?" Scales were painful to listen to. I knew it. Even my father knew it. But they were absolutely necessary to start with. I glanced at him on his pillows. He tried for a smile.

"Perhaps just the Mozart tonight, son."

I started playing my piece. I tried to make it sound the way it had in church. The way it seemed to swoop and fly, surprising me. Surprising everyone—the way Apa's special music had during Anya's picnic. I squeezed my eyes shut, imagining a huge space over my head, and a steeple. Then I let my mind go past the steeple and imagined a different space, a space in the safe summer woods open to the sky itself, with a huge mountain growing into the clouds just beyond my sight. With my eyes closed, it was almost possible. Finally I stopped.

Apa's own eyes were closed. I tucked my instrument into its case and stole upstairs.

Several nights after the doctor had been to visit a second time, I crept down the steps to deal with the lamps in the chicken coop. On the landing, I paused. Something was not right.

A very soft light flickered in the parlor. It outlined the shape sitting next to my father's sickbed. It was my mother. Her pale hair was undone and it spread softly around her shoulders, drifted over her nightgown.

"Anya?"

She held out her hand to me, blindly. I walked over and reached for it. I looked down at my father's face. "What's happened?"

But Anya didn't need to tell me. I knew. Apa was dead.

Dead as the Heller boys. Dead as the hatching chicks. Dead as the weasel. Dead.

Our neighbors were very kind. The whole town was. People I never remember talking to brought food. They took up a collection for us and even offered to look after the farm for a few days. An undertaker came and embalmed my father, right there in the parlor under the chandelier. Anya tried to keep us children outside in the cold air, but Sándor and I snuck back in. We spied from the hallway. Mr. Langley used an entire gallon of pink liquid to do the job.

"Why is it pink, Pista?" Sándor whispered.

I shook my head, unable to pull my eyes from what was happening. "I don't know."

"It's like changing the oil in an automobile," he started again. "Except for the color."

I wanted to scream at my brother to shut up, to forget about his cars and motors, but then I saw his face. I put my arm around his thin shoulders instead. He didn't shrug me off the way he usually did.

Next Anya dressed Apa in his best suit so that when the photographer came, he would look respectable in his coffin. I hovered in the background watching this, too. When she was finished, my mother bent over the wooden box and carefully smoothed my father's wonderful mustache.

After that was all accomplished, Anya finally turned to me. She'd been in a kind of daze for hours, but now her eyes cleared and she really saw me. She studied me, from my head to my boots.

"You've grown, Pista. You'll need a new shirt for the funeral this afternoon."

I was afraid to move. Afraid of anything that might come next. "What should I do?"

"Walk up to Mr. Martin's store for one."

I walked up that long road again. I did it slowly. My empty mind began filling with flashes of Apa. Apa working on his grand plans over the kitchen table. Apa planting rows of fruit trees in the field. Apa stacking little piles of money for an electric generator and an automobile. Apa just knowing that our farm would work. Apa was nearly always right.

I blinked away the images. The snow-covered trees were still on either side of me, still reaching out their branches. I didn't bother throwing a stone into the woods, against the darkness. Stones no longer held any power. From now on, I would have to make my own.

When I reached the store, old Mrs. Martin tried to smile for me.

"I'm so sorry. What can I do for you, Stephen?"

"I need a new shirt for my father's funeral, missus. On credit."

I walked home with the brown-paper-wrapped shirt under my arm. It was not the birthday present I would have chosen. But today I was eleven years old. The new man of the family needed a shirt that fit.